Doctor Schock transforms the carnival crowds into mindless pets with his tilt-a-whirl-brain-beam...and the whole world is next! Can the gang from Springton College stop the Doc *and* his private army? Step right up for rides, games, and *terror*!

Turn this book over for second complete novel

PRESENTS

Doctor Schock's
Carnival

BRET NELSON

Encyclopocalypse Publications
www.encyclopocalypse.com

Dr. Schock's Carnival
Giganticus!

Copyright © 2025 by Bret Nelson
All rights reserved.

ISBN: 978-1-966037-58-3
Cover Design by Grim Poppy Designs

Cover Layout by Sean Duregger
Interior design and formatting by Mark Alan Miller and Sean
Duregger
Edited by Mike Watt

Foreword

From 1961 to 1976, World Cinema Group fed the drive-in and dollar theater markets with a mix of low-budget monster flicks and exploitation films. Over the course of those 15 years, they released over 40 features, mostly based on pulp magazine stories and sci-fi novellas of the day.

The single owner and engine behind WCG was Harold J. Kerr (1917-1983).

His parents ran a linen supply house for restaurants, and though successful (one of their clients was Howard Johnson's), the business held no interest for Harold. Instead, he worked for his uncle, Leonard Kerr, who owned six movie theaters in the Midwest. Harold ran promotions for the chain.

Like all theaters, the chain struggled to compete with television in the 1950s. At the end of that decade, Harold J. Kerr moved to Hollywood, intent on "creating the product rather than projecting it." With some seed money from his parents and a guaranteed run at his uncle's theaters, Kerr produced his first feature using his apartment on Cherokee Avenue as an office.

Title card for Doctor Schock's Carnival *(1961)*

Doctor Schock's Carnival (1961) featured a lot of stock footage of tilt-a-whirls and a completely over-the-top performance by Vincent Barbi as the titular villain. Kerr found distribution beyond his uncle's screens. The picture ran in nine states and made a profit, thanks mainly to the title song by the then-popular rock band "The Pepper Grinders."

Original pressing, 45rpm single of The Pepper Grinders' song Doctor Schock! ((b-side: Training Wheels) *found in Kerr's home after his death in 1983. Most of the material stored there was in similar or worse condition.*

Kerr had seen his uncle trade movies on the sly with other theaters, dodging rental fees. It made him obsessive about keeping track of his films. He struck very few prints and moved them from venue to venue on tight schedules with tight books.

Each time a print ran at a new theater, it eroded a bit more. When there were too many scratches or gaps, what was left of the print was returned to World Cinema Group's offices on Gower Street in Hollywood. Kerr kept a hibachi in the alley behind the building where he burned the spent reels.

After their runs, the film masters were improperly stored at Kerr's home. They degraded, and now these films are lost.

Luckily, Kerr loved seeing stories in print. Many WCG pictures were adapted from pulp magazine tales or dime novellas. Original WCG pictures *became* pulp magazine tales or dime novellas after their theatrical runs.

So, with this volume we continue building an archive. The films may be lost, but the stories are not. Neither are the memories of the people who worked on them.

We are gathering them.

Mark Alan Miller (April, 2025)
Owner, Encyclopocalypse Publications

PRESENTS

Doctor Schock's
Carnival

1

All three members of the Springton Board of Supervisors met in the mayor's private office. They spent over an hour scrutinizing the galley proofs for the upcoming Springton County Fair's souvenir program.

"I still think we should keep the cover clean," said Robert Worthington, president of the Springton Commerce Bank and Trust. "We paid a lot of money for this artwork, and I can't see crowding it out with 'Sponsored by Barrington Birdies, makers of the world's most durable shuttlecocks.'"

"I am paying for the damn printing, so until either of you comes up with some cash I don't want to hear another word about it." Nigel Barrington didn't look at the other two board members. His eyes stayed locked on his cigarette as he mashed it into the ashtray, punctuating his statement.

"I get your point, Nigel," said James Remington, owner of four car dealerships and the newest board member. "It's 1959, and everyone knows that's the Springton Platinum Anniversary. Seventy years of the county *and* the fair. There's going to be big attendance, and we all want our names all over it. But this program design was already approved by the steering committee. How can we change it without another meeting? Especially when the change puts *your* business on the cover... you've already got the whole back page."

"My business is the largest employer in the damn county. And I'm the damn mayor of Springton, the damn county seat! Doesn't that rank me higher than the damn steering committee?" Barrington shook another cigarette out of the pack. "Besides, every one of the jerks on the stinking committee works for me at Barrington Birdies. I can't imagine they'd want it any other way."

"All right, all right," said Worthington. "We'll change the cover. I'll inform the committee *after* it's printed." He looked at a page of notes he'd been scribbling during the meeting. "So, we are two months from opening day. Parking and restrooms are covered, the insurance policy for the Springton 50 Car Race is in place, and the livestock clearances will come this Tuesday."

"Damn cows," said Barrington. "Brings in a bunch of hayseeds."

"It's a county fair. People expect farm animals."

"I know, I know. The idiots love those damn four-legged manure factories," said Barrington. "But milking contests and sheep shearing are relics. We should be using every inch of space to sell the future. Speaking of which, did we get those contracts back from that Schock fellow?"

"Yes," said Remmington. "Got them today, all signed. His group, Doctor Schock Diversions, will run the carnival area and all the concessions. Our cut is twenty percent."

"That is wonderful to hear," said Worthington, "And the utilities, all sorted?"

"No city power needed," said Remmington. "He's got a bunch of generator trucks, so he makes his own juice. They can't bring their own water, of course, but they've looked at the specs and the hookups at the fairgrounds will work fine. No changes needed."

"Well, it sounds like at least one thing is going right," said Barrington.

"Absolutely. This Doctor Schock comes highly recommended," said Remmington. "Terry Gresham, the assemblyman over in Kingsly County hired him for the Kingsly Rodeo last year. Said the carnival ran worry-free. Couldn't say enough good things about him."

———

By the second week of May, every store window and telephone pole in Springton displayed a poster for the event. Springton College senior Melvin Carstairs balanced a small stack of books and papers against his chest as he paused by the telephone pole outside Selkirk's Gas and Tune, reading about the wonders coming to town.

DON'T MISS THE SPRINGTON COUNTY FAIR'S
70TH ANNIVERSARY PLATINUM JUBILEE
*SPONSORED BY BARRINGTON BIRDIES, MAKERS OF THE
WORLD'S MOST DURABLE SHUTTLECOCKS*
CARNIVAL RIDES ● MIDWAY GAMES ● SPECTACULAR FOOD
● ANIMALS ANIMALS ANIMALS ● CONTESTS AND RAFFLES
EACH DAY
MAY 30TH ONLY:
TENTH ANNUAL SPRINGTON 50 CAR RACE
$1,000 TO THE WINNER!

With all the features listed, the car race was the

only thing on his mind. Carstairs imagined himself standing in the winner's circle with his friends holding a huge cardboard check.

Gosh. What we couldn't do with a thousand dollars, he thought.

Then his face got shoved into the poster. "Good morning, Carstairs," said a voice behind him. Even though his eyes were forced closed, he knew the giant palm holding his head belonged to Tank Barrington.

"Goub moaming," said Carstairs. The words were difficult with his face smushed. His mumble brought laughter from Tank and his two friends, Biff Worthington and Chad Remmington.

All sons of the community leaders. All ranking officers of the Mu Kau Mu fraternity. All dumber than a pile of scrap lumber.

Tank released his grip and used his other hand to spin Carstairs around. Melvin's books and papers tumbled to the ground.

"Oopsies," said Biff. "Looks like our boy Melvin had a catechism!"

Carstairs stooped to get his books. "Cata-*clysm*," he said.

Chad Remmington grabbed his shoulder and pulled him up. "We're here to remind you about our themes. You're gonna have a cata-*tastrophe* if we don't get them today."

"Right," said Tank. "We gotta have them themes for English Lit or we're sunk. And if we're sunk, you're sunk, too."

"You'll have them," said Carstairs. "Be under the tower clock in the quad at three. Little hand on the three, big hand on the twelve."

"Funny, Melvin," said Biff. "You're gonna make me laugh so hard I have a compulsion. See you at three." The trio walked off, laughing and recounting the events from a minute ago.

"Con-*vulsion*," whispered Carstairs, bending to pick up his books. He jumped a bit as a slender hand passed him some papers that had flown down the street.

"Hey Cosine, these got away from you." The hand belonged to Christy Trunkett, daughter of the dean.

Being a wonder with numbers, Melvin Carstairs was known as "Cosine" to his friends. He was glad to see Christy, but not so glad she witnessed his humiliation. They'd been dating for close to a year.

They gathered up his things then walked together, talking about the hot rod Cosine had entered to race in the Springton 50.

———

Many miles away, Sheldon Phlipworth adjusted his spectacles and examined the single sheet of paper on his clipboard. His finger moved down a neat column of checked boxes. Each represented a task completed. Twenty people hovered nearby, waiting for instructions.

"Load out is complete," said Phlipworth. He dropped the clipboard into his briefcase. "Do a final check on every tie-down, door keeper, and gate. We roll out in thirty minutes." Without a word spoken, each of the people moved as ordered along the convoy of trucks carrying Doctor Schock's Carnival.

Phlipworth gripped his briefcase tight and walked the length of the convoy to the motorhome at the far end. He knocked and a melodic voice answered. "Is that you Phlipworth?"

"Yes, Doctor Schock."

"It's open."

The interior of the motorhome was well appointed, rivaling any big-city apartment. Doctor Eduard Schock stood at a chalkboard filled with calculations. White powder streaked the lower sleeves of his paisley housecoat. "We've finished roughing out the new energy requirements for the brain beam. Pumm Pumm is taking it all down. Have a seat."

The large, chenille cabriole leg sofa looked inviting indeed. Phlipworth had been wrangling the load out of Schock's two-acre carnival all day. He sat for the first time in several hours and immediately felt some tension melt away. A great hand patted his shoulder as he heard a "hurmph."

He squeezed the hand and smiled at his couch mate, a 300-pound gorilla wearing a suit and tie. "Good to see you, Pumm Pumm," said Phlipworth.

Pumm Pumm gave him a nod and returned to copying equations and diagrams in a large composition book.

"Are we on time?" asked Doctor Schock. "It is two days to Springton, in the best case. History will not wait."

"And in thirty minutes we will be on our way," said Phlipworth. He held up his briefcase. "I've prepared dossiers on the wealthiest citizens and others likely to help us. I can step you through them once we're on the road. It will pass the hours on the drive."

"Yes. A good use of our time," said the doctor.

Pumm Pumm huffed and held up a thumb.

And in thirty minutes, the trucks roared their engines, and the convoy pulled away from the Monterey Sawdust Festival grounds, bound for the interstate toward Springton County.

2

"Looks like you're away, Dean Trunkett," said James Remmington.

The dean's ball was a full ten feet farther from the cup than anyone else's. "So I am," said Trunkett, approaching the green with his putter in hand. "Thank you, Mr. Remmington."

"Please, call me Jimmy."

There was a time when everyone thought Jimmy "Jim Jam" Remmington, star defensive lineman for the Springton Sultans, would be drafted by the National Football League. An injury during his last season at the college closed the door on a sports career.

That was all decades ago. Now, his car dealerships for Ford, Chevy, Chrysler, and luxury models moved more inventory than any other in the state. His face was on billboards all over the county with giant letters reading *NO pressure. NO gimmicks. NO reasonable offer refused.*

Dean Eugene Trunkett's confident putt dropped right in the cup. He raised his putter with a tiny flourish. "The old equalizer. Long game is falling apart these days, but at least I don't embarrass myself on the greens."

"Well done," said Nigel Barrington. "Glad you could join us this morning."

"Yes," said Robert Worthington. "Nice day for it." He dropped to one knee behind his ball and tried to read the break. "By the way, did you get a chance to look over the proposal we sent?"

"I did, I did." Trunkett stepped to the side of the green, removing his shadow from Worthington's line. "I'll send it along to the planning committee, but I don't think they'll like it. I've told you before, building a new science campus is the only expansion they are interested in. We already have a stadium."

All paused as Worthington took his putt. The ball rolled well past the target.

"It's still you," said the dean. Worthington grimaced and made his way to the other side of the green.

"That stadium hasn't had a single improvement since Jim Jam's day," said Barrington.

"And there were cracks in the plaster back then," said Remmington.

"If you're going to build on college land, expand your sports complex," said Barrington. "It can't miss. New fields for baseball and lacrosse. Get the track covered in urethane. Add better parking and update the stadium while you're at it. We've already floated the idea to a couple of sponsors. They love it. Can't wait to kick in some funding. This will really help the city of Springton grow."

"Our science curriculum is attracting sponsors as well," said Trunkett. "We've got computer companies, chemical manufacturers, and even the space program offering scholarships."

"But that won't sell any tickets," said Remmington. "Science costs a lot of money. Sports makes a lot of money."

"That's right," said Worthington, then he missed his putt again.

After the round, Dean Trunkett honked his horn and waved to the others through his car window as he left the Springton Links Country Club. Once he was out of sight, Nigel Barrington threw his golf bag into the trunk of his Cadillac. "Damn that man! Short-sighted! Obstinate!"

"And ungrateful," said Worthington.

"Exactly," said Barrington, shaking a finger. "Ungrateful! Why did we ever invite him to play at this club in the first place?"

"He did say 'thank you,'" said Remmington.

"We don't need his thanks, we need him to get our proposal signed," said Worthington. "We're going to miss out on a fortune if this science campus goes through."

"You're right," said Remmington. "He seems certain the sports complex doesn't stand a chance with the planning committee."

"When are they supposed to make it all final?" asked Barrington.

"The loans will go through my bank," said Worthington. "That won't be for at least another sixty days."

"Then we've got sixty days to figure out how to change their minds," said Remmington.

"Or force their hand," said Barrington.

Melvin Carstairs had the same pair of study partners since high school - Stanley Terklehopper and

Josephine Selkirk. They were his closest friends, and the trio called themselves the *Lab Rats*.

Most of the time, Stanley "Tubes" Terklehopper kept his mop of curly red hair tucked inside an old Derby hat. Because most of the time he hovered over beakers and Bunsen burners that threatened his hair with ignition.

Chemistry came to him as easily as breathing, but he was often overconfident in his ability to control the elements. During his sophomore year, he had to shave his head after using too much potassium chlorate in an experiment. When it went POOF, it turned his shaggy mane bright blue. Fortunately, it grew back quickly in its original color.

Josephine "Sparky" Selkirk had an innate understanding of electricity, wire, and gadgets rivaling her father's. Her dad was Emerson Selkirk, owner of Selkirk's Gas and Tune.

The Lab Rats had been spending most of their time in a large shed behind the service station. Earlier this year, the elder Selkirk agreed to let them have the space and the rusted remains of a 1949 Nash Airflyte to use for their senior project.

They had convinced the science department chairs to let them work together on a senior project of their own design. A project to demonstrate advances in mathematics, electronics, chemistry, and physics all working together.

Cosine, Sparky, and Tubes also hoped the project would win the Springton 50 auto race. The project was an automobile they called the Pixii. They didn't give it that name because it was magical. The car was named for Hippolyte Pixii, a French scientist and inventor from the early 1800s who started humanity on the road to understanding electromagnetic induction.

They had already fixed up the car. Although it

didn't have custom paint or chrome, it was clean. And it ran like nobody's business.

But underneath, the Pixii had an experimental motor and drive system unlike anything else, and if it worked it would change the world. Trouble was, it wasn't working yet, and the race was less than a week away.

The doors of the shed flew open. Out poured clouds of green smoke and three young scientists, coughing and waving their hands in front of their faces.

"The skylight is open. It'll air out in a minute," said Tubes, choking. "Eventually we'll run out of wrong formulas, then we'll have the right one."

"We should have run this test outdoors," said Sparky between deep breaths. "We're lucky the explosion was small. If we blow up this shed, Dad will kill me."

"If the explosion's big enough to blow up the shed, your pop won't need to kill you," said Cosine. "We'd be dead already. I wrote out very specific measures for you, Tubes. Didn't use them, did you?"

"Your calculations were looking for the safest formulation," said Tubes, checking his sleeves for burns. "I'm looking for the most powerful formulation. So yes, I changed some things. Specifically, I added a few more grains of zinc and three more drops of methyl methacrylate."

"Three drops!" said Cosine. "No wonder it went critical."

"Adding more than you're supposed to is the only way to find out how much *is* too much," said Tubes. "The smoke's already clear. Let's see what we've got."

With careful steps, they went back inside the shed. Sparky's hand swept the sheet metal door, and a tiny blue arc popped from her fingers. "Ouch," she said.

"We've got to figure out a way to ground you," said Tubes. "I can't count the number of times you've shocked me today."

"Electricity is in my blood," said Sparky. She examined the equipment in the shed. "Everything's standing. Must not have been an explosion. Just a big, noisy reaction with lots of green smoke."

Cosine eyed the large beaker at the end of their distillation rig. It was half-filled with fluid. "Looks like the reaction is finished. Is this stuff thicker than the last batch?"

Tubes pulled the goggles off his derby and snapped them over his eyes. He scrutinized the beaker. "It is thicker. Purple color is deeper, too." He lifted it off the cradle and shook it. Cosine and Sparky ducked for cover.

"Tubes!" said Sparky. "Are you nuts?"

"Calm down, I'm only making sure it's stable," he said. "Let's give it a spin in the prototype."

He measured out four ounces of the purple concoction and poured it into the reservoir of a raw machine bolted to the table. Sparky donned her goggles and checked connections on the meters she'd attached to it.

Cosine pulled on his goggles and blew a puff of green dust off his clipboard. "I'm really looking forward to the day we get to install this in the car," he said. "Hit it."

Tubes flicked a toggle switch and pulled a small cord. The machine whirred to life, hardly making a sound.

"Hot dog, look at that," said Tubes. "The burn is way more efficient. This might be our day."

Cosine marked down meter readings on his clipboard. "Maybe... these are the best numbers yet."

Those numbers dropped after ten minutes. "Oh

no, look at the third dial," said Sparky. The needle was moving left. The wrong direction.

"Viscosity is breaking down," said Tubes. "So close. I think I know what to adjust, then this fuel additive will turn regular old gasoline into rocket fuel!"

"I think you're right," said Cosine, reviewing the rest of the numbers. "This batch is doing everything we want, but we need to find a way to keep it from thinning out." He caught a glimpse of his watch. "Rats, it's getting near three. I've got to get to the quad and hand off those themes to Barrington, Remmington, and Worthington."

"Let's call them the *Doltingtons*," said Tubes. "It's shorter."

"Oh, I like it a lot. Good name for those cinder blocks," said Sparky. "We'll keep working on this, Cosine. You can go say *hi* to the Doltingtons."

———

Over on Greek Row, a few blocks from the Springton College campus, Chad Remmington, Tank Barrington, and Biff Worthington sat on the porch of the Mu Kau Mu fraternity house. Each of them had an envelope from Melvin Carstairs with a theme inside. Biff conducted a line-by-line review of his.

"What are you doing?" asked Chad, peeling the label off his beer bottle.

"Looking for traps," said Biff. He put his finger on the page to hold his place while he addressed the others. "Those guys might try to hide something in here to get me in trouble."

"A trap?" said Tank. "That sounds goofy."

Biff thumped the page and spun it around for the others to see. "Aha! Look, right here. This word –

diplomacy – they spelled it with an '8' instead of 'e-y.' Trying to make me look like a moron."

"They gotta put mistakes in," said Chad. "Little ones. Otherwise, it won't look like you wrote it."

"Yeah, you moron," said Tank. "Besides, those eggheads won't ever shaft us."

"He's right," said Chad. "Your dad owns the mortgage on Selkirk's gas station. And Terklehopper's pop works for Tank's old man at the birdie factory. Same with Carstairs. They don't want any trouble for their families, so they won't cause any trouble for us.

"Yeah, but if push comes to shove nothing's gonna happen," said Biff. "There's no way my dad would mess with their folks on my say so. He never listens to me."

"Same here," said Tank. "Heck, if I asked Pop to fire someone, he'd probably give them a raise just to spite me."

"We know that, but they don't," said Chad. "As long as they don't, we'll ride this homework train as far as it will go." He spent a moment admiring the job he'd done clearing his beer bottle of paper and adhesive. Suddenly, he brightened.

"Hey! Speaking of rides," he said, "My old man took delivery on our car today. He's having *Remmington Motors* painted on the hood and the doors."

Chad pulled a brochure from his book-bag. "Feast your eyes, it's a Dodge D-500."

"Never heard of it," said Biff. "Can't he get us a Corvette?"

"This is better." With another dig into the book-bag, Chad produced the current issue of *Life Magazine*, folded back to reveal a full-page ad for their car. "See, this is the one we're getting," he said. "But ours is red."

"Holy cow, that's sharp," said Tank. "And look at the picture - it's blowing *past* a Corvette!"

"Uphill!" said Biff. He grabbed the magazine and inspected the ad. "Wait a minute, it's only a drawing. They can draw anything. They can make it look like it's passing a jet."

"They can't put it in an ad if it's not true, right?" said Chad.

"Yeah, he's right," said Tank. "That's like a law. It's gotta be true."

"Oh. That makes sense," said Biff. "And it's really fast?"

Chad flipped to the appropriate page of the brochure. "It's a new *kind* of fast. The D-500 has this gadget called an Electrojector!"

"Electrojector? Sounds like something outta *Space Patrol*," said Tank. He and Biff crowded around the brochure and pretended to understand what the specifications meant.

"My old man says it's the way of the future," said Chad. "This doodad uses a computer to keep the fuel mix right and injects the gas straight into the engine. The car has a mechanical brain so it goes faster!"

"Hot dog!" said Biff. "Springton 50, here we come!"

3

In most cities, the "fairgrounds" were simply a few acres of asphalt and dirt. In Springton, the grounds included well maintained parking areas and public restrooms because they shared space with the Springton Speedway.

Opened twelve years ago, the Speedway featured a two-mile oval track and a three-mile infield road course boasting twenty-one turns. The final event for this year's fair was the tenth annual Springton 50. This was a non-pro event where local garages, hot-rodders, and gearheads ran their cars twenty-five laps around the oval for the chance to win a $1,000 prize. Nearly one hundred drivers entered, and twenty were picked in a random drawing to participate in the race.

Among those chosen were Melvin Carstairs' Pixii and the Remmington Racer.

———

Riley Chance had been manager of the Springton County Fairgrounds for over a decade. He'd spent most of yesterday morning making certain the plumbing and electrical terminations were trouble-free. He'd spent yesterday afternoon driving a water truck over the dirt areas to make sure the dust stayed down when Doctor Schock's Carnival arrived to load in this morning.

The prep order provided by Mr. Phlipworth, Schock's advance man, was startling in its simplicity. The only requirement was a single stake driven into the ground at a point marked on a provided schematic.

Chance hired a surveyor to confirm the stake's position. "Only one thing to do and I'll be damned if I do it wrong," he thought.

Equally startling was the scheduling. Schock's crew needed a single day to load in their two-acre carnival. Riley Chance was looking forward to seeing how they'd do it.

As the sun rose over the fairgrounds, a single car approached, a big Cadillac. Jimmy Remmington had come to see Schock's arrival and make certain Springton had held up their side of the contract.

"Morning Mr. Remmington," said Chance. "Ought to see them coming over the rise any time now. They seem pretty organized."

"Gotta be better than the low-rent crew we hired to run the carnival last year," said Remmington. "Half the rides didn't work and the ones that did were shaky and loose."

"They expect to get the heavy work done in a day. Hats off to them if they can pull it off, but I doubt it," said Chance. "Didn't even want to hire local help for their load in. Said they got enough people to cover it."

"This Schock fellow is very smart. I bet they get it done on time."

"As I say, hats off if they do. The advance man, what's his name again? Phillips?"

"Phlipworth."

"That's the one. Said he'd be here at seven and... hang on, this must be him."

An International Harvester D-Series truck hauling a custom trailer pulled into the fairgrounds. The trailer was painted to look like an old wooden show wagon with banners reading *Doctor Schock's Carnival* all around.

Sheldon Phlipworth was behind the wheel. He pulled up alongside Remmington and Chance. "Good morning," he said, looking past them to the stake in the ground. He held up a schematic drawing and pointed to a small red dot. "That stake marks this location, correct?"

"Yes it does, Mr. Phlipworth," said Chance. "Ten feet east from the center of the fairgrounds."

"Marvelous. Thank you very much, Mr. Chance."

"Good golly, Mr. Phlipworth, this a '38, isn't it?" said Remmington.

"Good eye, Mr. Remmington. It is indeed."

"Well, it looks like it rolled out of the showroom yesterday. And listen to that engine! Not a ping or a miss."

"We take care of our equipment, Mr. Remmington. Thank you for noticing," said Phlipworth. "May I trouble you gentlemen to stand well out of the way. My people have much to do." He clutched the wheel and with three assured turns, Phlipworth backed up the trailer until the center of the bumper rested precisely against the stake. He shut down the engine and engaged the brake. Then he went around to the trailer's door.

"Do you need any help with anything?" asked Chance.

"No, thank you Mr. Chance. You've been very helpful indeed. Thank you again." With a great tug, he opened the back door of the trailer. Six people hopped out and grabbed handles on one of the trailer's side panels. With a twist and a tug, the panel came off and they stored it in the back of the International Harvester truck. The other side panels were removed and stored in the same way.

There were more people inside of what had now become an open-air control booth for the carnival. Workstations lined a waist-high railing and tables were covered with drawings and diagrams. Three teams jumped to work pulling on tape measures and passing around schematics. They drove stakes and stretched different colors of flagging tape to mark the future location of midway booths, concession stands, and rides.

Phlipworth disconnected the truck from the trailer and drove it to the farthest point on the property. By the time he walked back to the control booth, most of the stakes were in place and the first of the big trucks were coming down the road.

———

Half an hour later, Remmington had breakfast at the Sunshine Diner with Robert Worthington.

"You should get down there and have a look," said Remmington between bites of his *Sunrise Sausage Scramble*. "It's all going up so quick. And no confusion, no pauses. Like a drill team. Amazing!"

"I've got better things to do than watch a bunch of sweaty roustabouts pull on ropes," said Worthington, gulping down the last of his coffee. "Besides, I've got to get back to the main branch. Mr. Phlipworth is coming in with a sizable deposit later this morning."

"They've got an account at your bank?"

"Opened it last week with $5,000. All in hundreds. Said they always have an account at a local bank where they're working." Worthington snatched up their breakfast check. "This carnival stuff is a cash business. Their safe got knocked over years ago, so they'd rather keep their lucre in our vault." He spent a moment reviewing the waitress' math.

"You want me to help?" asked Remmington.

"I've got it," said Worthington. "You get the tip. When the fair closes, they'll close out their account. But until then, my books look great! Aces, Jimmy! Aces!"

————

An hour and a half before sunset, Doctor Schock's Carnival stood completed, like it had always been there. Schock's people were still calibrating the mechanical midway games and testing the rides, but the building portion of the load in was finished. Structures were all in place with their power lines running to the generator cabins and their audio lines running to the broadcast booths.

Pumm Pumm supervised the finishing work. He wore a collar and tie with his sleeves rolled up and a hard-hat on his head. He used hand signals and body language to give orders to the crew and tracked their progress on a series of clipboards hanging in the control booth.

That booth had moved from its earlier location – vertically. Now, it topped a fifty-foot-high tower with views of the entire two-acre carnival.

None of the crew reacted to the ape being charge. For them, it was just another day. But the manager of the fairgrounds, Riley Chance, thought it had to be a gag. *Guy in a monkey costume, like in the movies*, he thought. *Get the people talking early. Come and see the gorilla in charge. That Schock's a genius.*

He was making his way to the parking area. In an hour he'd be meeting Sheriff Mort Dodson there to talk about patrols around the fair. On his way, walking the fence line, he found three people watching the work below, each with their own set of binoculars.

"I'm telling you guys," said Sparky Selkirk, "that is a real gorilla."

"Can't be," said Tubes.

"I can't tell," said Cosine. "Can we get any closer?"

"Sorry folks. Until tomorrow night this is as close as you get," said Chance. All the binoculars came down.

"Hello Mr. Chance," said Sparky.

"Josephine Selkirk, thought it was you spying on that monkey." Chance smiled. "Carstairs, Terklehopper. Good to see you. How long have you been here?"

"We wanted to watch them set up the rides," said Cosine. "The way they designed the tilt-a-whirl to fold up and fit on one truck is amazing."

"Yeah," said Tubes. "Then we saw the guy in an ape suit, and we've been watching him ever since."

"It's not a suit," said Sparky, looking through the binoculars again. "There's too much detail. And he behaves like a gorilla even when no one is around. Have you met him, Mr. Chance?"

"No, but I have met the carnival's advance man, Mr. Phlipworth. He says it's a real monkey. I say it's the business." Chance looked toward the empty parking area. The sheriff's cruiser wasn't there yet.

"You three can stay here and watch, but once the sun goes down they don't want anyone around," said Chance. "Sheriff's going to leave an officer to patrol the area overnight. I'm headed to meet them now."

"We'll clear out soon, Mr. Chance," said Cosine.

"Gotta do some more work on our car tonight, anyways."

———

Officer Daniel Cleary didn't mind overnight shifts. Springton was quiet at night, unless the college brats were working a prank.

Tonight, all he had to do was keep an eye on the carnival.

Earlier, Sheldon Phlipworth introduced him to a dozen people in dark blue jackets. They were Doctor Schock's security detail. They didn't have the authority to manhandle anyone or arrest them, but their high visibility prevented a lot of problems. Tonight, and every night after the carnival closed for the evening, they held stations along the fence line and in the parking area.

With the extra help, Officer Cleary's job became even simpler. After a few hours of his uneventful shift, Phlipworth appeared and invited Officer Cleary on a tour. A chance to see some of the rides being lit up and tested out.

Cleary welcomed the opportunity, with a caveat. "Is the gorilla guy still around? He kinda spooks me."

"Pumm Pumm is a wonder," said Phlipworth. "He's round back at the moment, but you should meet him properly. I think you'll get along quite well. Most people like him very much."

"Uhm, maybe later," said Cleary.

Their walk around the grounds paused where a red and black ride sparked to life with lights and music. "Ah, up and running," said Phlipworth. "This, Officer Cleary, is the *Rocking Riot*. It started life as a basic tilt-a-whirl. Doctor Schock added custom paint in bright red and shiny black, dotted with silver music notes. The top has a clear plexidome with neon tubes of all colors running up the sides. It's meant to resemble a mad jukebox, with the riders' cars balanced on top of the records."

"It does at that," said Cleary. "These spinning rides aren't for me though. When I was a kid the merry-go-round at the playground caused me fits."

"We have a playground-inspired attraction over here - *Schock's Sling*," said Phlipworth. "Chains suspend your leather-strap seats from a metal rod above, but the similarities between this and the swing set at your community park end there."

"Let me guess," said Cleary. "Another spinner?"

"I afraid so. The metal rod holding the chains is one of many spokes in the enormous wheel up there. Once the ride starts, the wheel rises twenty feet in the air," Phlipworth gave a nod to the operator, who set the ride in motion.

Phlipworth narrated as *Schock's Sling* rose. "At full height, with the riders' feet dangling, the wheel turns. The speed increases, the swings fan out. And when the giggles and tight stomachs begin to get used to all this, the whole thing cants to one side. Riders get alternating views of the sky and the ground as they whirl about like a stone in a sling, waiting to be launched at the forehead of Goliath."

"Goodness," said Cleary. "You sure have a way with words, Mr. Phlipworth."

"Thank you. Over here is a ride you can actually enjoy. They've lit up our pride and joy, you see?

"I can see it," said Cleary. "How could I miss it? It's huge."

"The *Grand Ferris Wheel* stands over 200 feet tall," said Phlipworth. "Visible from anywhere in Springton, most likely. It was built in 1902 for the Canada World Exposition, and it toured up there for decades until Doctor Schock purchased it. It took some work to refurbish the thing as the previous owner didn't keep it up well. But now, like all the other gear here at the carnival, it's kept in top form. We've modernized the motor and wiring, so I'd wager it's better than new."

At the back of the carnival, a large facade made of plywood and canvas featured an enormous mural. It depicted larger than life attractions stretching on for miles and kept the generators, trucks, storage containers, and other mundane structures out of sight.

"Here's something most of our attendees will not see," said Phlipworth. "A real look behind the scenes." He escorted Cleary to a door hidden in the mural.

"That's clever. I thought it was part of the picture," said Cleary.

"This door leads backstage," said Phlipworth. "Come with me."

Officer Cleary walked through the painted door. One hour later, he emerged and returned to his patrol.

He was a changed man.

4

Opening day of the Springton County Fair's 70th Anniversary Platinum Jubilee started with a parade featuring the Springton High Marching Band and the local Shriners buzzing about in tiny cars. Mayor Barrington and his family waved from a Cadillac Series 62 convertible provided by Remmington Luxury Motors.

Like every year, the parade ended with the local equestrian group leading the crowd to the fair gates, which swung wide after a short speech from the mayor.

The farm and hayride areas were open. Pies were eaten competitively. Jams were judged. Pumpkins were weighed. Ribbons were awarded. Young and old alike watched milking and shearing and horseshoeing. A real blacksmith hammered out real horseshoes.

Piglets raced around a tiny track every hour on the hour. Teams rotated onto a badminton court attempting to set the record for the longest volley with a single shuttlecock. Said shuttlecock was provided, along with the other gear, by Barrington Birdies (the event's sponsor).

At the eastern edge of the farm area, another gate

isolated Doctor Schock's Carnival from the rest of the fair. People lined up at the booths buying sheets of tickets for the opening.

Schock insisted on holding the launch after sundown. The public's first look at the carnival had to feature all the lights, thousands of them. For the rest of the run, the carnival's hours were 10am to 10pm each day, but tonight's opening had to be special.

All three members of the Springton Board of Supervisors would be there shortly after the carnival opened this evening. They had been invited to dine with Doctor Schock and discuss a business proposal.

———

When the sun fell behind the rise in Springton County, the dark came on fast. Crowds were gathered at the gates as sunset approached, but the carnival was still and unlit.

Then, the moment the darkness arrived, two bold spotlights sparked to life and illuminated the tower above the carnival grounds. Prerecorded fanfare played over the public address system and the crowd erupted into cheers. On the tower's roof, at the intersection of the spotlights, stood Doctor Eduard Schock. He wore a red cutaway coat and an impossibly tall stovepipe hat.

He spoke into a large bullhorn painted with red and white stripes. "Good evening one and all. I am Doctor Schock, and welcome to my carnival."

The crowd went wild. Some of the parents had trouble keeping their younger children in check, and wished he'd stop talking and let everyone in.

But his speech continued. "I said *my* carnival, but it is actually yours. A place created for you. A place where you can win games of skill and eat delicious treats. Where you can explore a haunted castle, take a boat ride, or sail through the air at dizzying speeds."

The doctor took in a deep breath and raised his tall hat with his free hand.

"Or, if you'd rather," he declared, "you can take in the sights!"

In the booth below, Pumm Pumm threw the main switch. All at once, every light in the carnival glowed bright. Every sound blared and every ride began to move. What was darkness a second before became a tantalizing display of blinking jellybean colors, beckoning all.

The crowd fell silent for a moment, then cheered again as the doctor's blue-jacketed security people swung the gates wide.

"Welcome, everyone! Please come inside," said the doctor. "Mind how you go, no need to crowd. I'll see you again soon!"

The spotlights went out and Doctor Schock moved carefully into the control booth on top of the tower. There, he joined Pumm Pumm and watched the crowds on an array of video screens. Hidden cameras provided views all over the park. "Those new settings of yours are a wonder, old friend," he said. "Look at them. They are already awash in my will."

The gorilla nodded and raised his hand in a thumbs up.

Below, every person in range of the lights and sounds carried a look of ease and happiness, unaware of the low-intensity brain beams emitted by the *Grand Ferris Wheel*. Even the smaller children had settled. The throngs of people strolled through the gates without tussling, without crowding. Each made room for the other and managed an orderly pace into Doctor Schock's Carnival.

———

Ages ago, Sheldon Phlipworth was a barker at Coney Island. He'd pull together a crowd from passers by on the boardwalk and lead them on a walking tour through The Ocean Marvels Museum. He'd narrate as patrons ogled a glass case containing the remains of an actual mermaid. In the next room, they'd find a row of ancient driftwood planks. Experts at the Cairo Historical Institute confirmed they were the last remnants of Cleopatra's Barge.

People paid a quarter to take the fifteen-minute trip through half a dozen Ocean Marvels. It was up to Phlipworth to spin tales so full of fun and wonder that even if the mermaid was unconvincing, the customers still felt they got value for their two bits.

He used those talents as he led all three members of the Springton Board of Supervisors on a tour of Doctor Schock's Carnival.

"That had to be a trick, Mr. Phlipworth," said Robert Worthington. "The bird won every time."

"I assure you, Mr. Worthington, it is no trick. I'm not sure how he acquired the skill, but Mycroft is the only budgie in the world who plays checkers so well."

"I'm with you, Bob," said Nigel Barrington. A cigarette dangled from his lip as he pawed through his pockets searching for his lighter. "It's a trick, but it sure is a good one. And I know my birdies!"

That got laughs all around. Phlipworth produced a book of matches with the carnival's logo. He handed out the matchbooks to each of the men as they walked along the *Thrillzone*, an area dedicated to rides with spins, drops, and speed. The soundscape was a mix of whirs and clatters from the machinery and happy screams from the riders.

"I trust the ticket books found their way to you," said Phlipworth.

"Yes, thanks," said James Remmington. "Our boys are going to make good use of them."

"Excellent," said Phlipworth. "You know, we have a new attraction in need of testing. Would your sons be interested in some work? Pays well, and it's just a few hours right here. Nothing dangerous. We'd like some fresh eyes to look at the thing and tell us what they think of it."

"Sounds terrific," said Worthington.

"Excellent," said Phlipworth. "Have them here tomorrow morning around 11:00am."

"Marvelous," said Barrington. They stopped for a moment as a large group crossed their path. "Look at this crowd. Bet there's a lot of money moving around."

"Here are some numbers to consider," said Phlipworth. "A sheet of eight tickets sells for one dollar. Some rides cost one ticket, but the bigger rides cost four, like the *Schocking Speedster* here."

A car on the coaster over their heads rolled straight down then turned sharp. "Wow," said Remmington. "That thing's quick!"

"Indeed," said Phlipworth. "Two big drops and two sideways corkscrews with some stretches of fast track in between. It lasts two and a half minutes and when it's over, many riders get right back in line for another run."

"Looks like eight people in every car," said Worthington. "If my math is right, you're making four bucks every time a car goes off."

"Yes. And there are multiple cars. This single attraction generates well over $300 per hour."

"That thing makes more than my lawyer," said Barrington. "You've got quite a racket here."

29

"There is a bargain available," said Phlipworth. "A book of tickets runs ten dollars for a dozen sheets, that's like getting sixteen tickets for free. The customers who purchase these books tend to stay on site longer. They save on tickets but spend more money at the concession stands and buying souvenirs."

"Can you still have fun without a lot of tickets?" asked Remmington.

"Certainly." Phlipworth led them to a huge staircase with a steady line of youngsters making their way to the top. "This is our most popular one-ticket ride. It is the world's largest eight-lane slide. We call it *Freefall*."

"Is it really the world's largest?" asked Barrington.

"No one has disputed the claim," said Phlipworth.

"What are those kids carrying?" asked Worthington.

"Here, at the entrance, you are given a gunnysack in exchange for your ticket," said Phlipworth. "Once you make the four-story climb and sit in your lane, you'll shimmy into the burlap bag until it comes up to your waist."

Worthington squinted, trying to see the top of the slide. "Why do I need to be in a sack?"

"You are about to battle gravity itself. The material will keep your shoes from slowing you down. And many wear skirts, shorts, or capris, exposing their legs. These lowly gunnysacks prevent burns and scrapes. They were once storage for dry goods, now they are a life-saving sheath for the tender skin of America's youth."

"My word," said Barrington, with a chuckle. "You lay it on thick, don't you Mr. Phlipworth?"

"Part of the job, Mr. Barrington." He returned to his description of *Freefall*. "As I was saying, after you've tucked yourself in the sack one of our helpful employees provides a gentle push and off you go. If you and your friends occupy several lanes, the push comes 'on three' so you can race. I'm told it's great fun."

"My boy is gonna love that," said Worthington. "He's very competitive."

———

"I'm gonna beat every one of these games," said Biff Worthington, standing in the center of the midway. "Look over there! They got a balloon race. You know, you aim this squirt gun in a clown's mouth and a balloon grows out of his head."

"I don't like that one," said Tank. "I always get the weak gun. Let's knock over those milk bottles. I can win that."

"I wanna pop balloons with darts," said Chad. "Oh, even better, there's the shooting gallery! Let's start there."

"Let's start anywhere," said Tank between handfuls of popcorn. "So far we've been standing here yacking."

Schock and Pumm Pumm had been watching the boys from their perch in the control booth above the carnival. "These three. Sons of our special guests," said the doctor. "They are so obstinate, so filled with their own lusts it blocks our low-grade beam. But we knew that, didn't we old friend?"

Pumm Pumm nodded and shrugged.

"That's right, Pumm Pumm. Extremely dim people or extremely smart ones will need a more intense treatment." The doctor checked his pocket watch. "Goodness, our guests are due in an hour. We'd better get back home. History will not abide tardiness."

31

———

The Doltingtons continued negotiating about what to do next.

"Criminy! Over by the snack shack, it's that thing!" said Biff.

"There's a hundred *things* over there," said Chad.

"You know, the thing," said Biff. "What do you call it? With the mallet where you ring the bell?"

"It's called *Ring the Bell*, you moron," said Chad.

"Well, I'm gonna ring it like crazy. Probably knock the stupid bell right off the top."

After several failed attempts, Biff became convinced the game was rigged. Then Tank rang the bell on his first try.

———

Phlipworth led his guests through the hidden door in the mural to the back area of the carnival. There, he pointed out an ornate canvas structure. "Doctor Schock's quarters are in that marquee tent," he said. "It is where you shall dine. Please, follow me."

"Will you be joining us?" asked Remmington.

"Sadly no, I have duties elsewhere." Phlipworth escorted them inside the tent. "Doctor, your guests have arrived. This is Mr. Worthington, Mr. Barrington, and Mr. Remmington."

"Excellent," said Schock, emerging from behind a vast writing desk. "Welcome, gentlemen." The doctor had swapped his ringmaster garb for a charcoal suit. A madras ascot of burgundy and orange lay tucked under his chin.

"I'm certain I'll see you all again soon," said Phlipworth, leaving. Everyone said their goodbyes, then the men had a good look at the interior of the tent.

"Holy cow," said Worthington. "This is grand. Just grand."

"Camping is the only time I've been in a tent," said Remmington. "Nothing like this."

They found themselves in an ample drawing room. Art Nouveau furniture, lush carpeting, and fine sculptures surrounded them. A full-size dining area waited on the other side of an ornately painted divider screen.

"Have a seat and make yourselves comfortable," said Schock, shaking hands. "Pumm Pumm, please see to our guests."

None of the men had noticed the gorilla laying out place settings past the divider. He was dressed in an oversized gray drape suit. His thin, violet tie pulled into a sharp Full Windsor knot. The ape trotted to the wet bar near Schock's desk and waited for orders as Worthington, Remmington, and Barrington cautiously lowered themselves into overstuffed easy chairs.

"What's your pleasure, gentlemen?" asked Schock, easing onto a velvet chaise. "I'm having a scotch, neat."

"Eh, same for me, thanks," said Barrington.

"Splash of soda in mine, please," said Worthington. "What did you say his name was?"

"Pumm Pumm," said Schock.

"Can Pumm Pumm make a martini?" asked Remmington. "I've only met two *humans* who can do it right."

Pumm Pumm rolled his eyes, then gathered the cocktail shaker and other tools. He held up two bottles, one gin and one vodka.

That got a grin out of Remmington. "Gin please. Dry, with two olives." The ape nodded and got to work.

"That's quite a butler you've got there, Doctor," said Barrington.

"He's much more than a servant, Mr. Barrington. Pumm Pumm and I have been together for quite some time. I rescued him from a lab in Europe. The so-called scientists there took him out of the Congo when he was a child and did… things to his brain. Astonishing results, but they didn't treat him well."

Though he was trying not to listen, Pumm Pumm heard every word. Thinking of those days still made him shudder.

Schock noticed. "Let's not speak of it, bad memories I'm afraid. Sorry old friend."

The gorilla shrugged as he carried a tray of drinks around the room. After everyone took theirs, one remained - an old fashioned with extra fruit. Pumm Pumm made it for himself. He raised his drink, looked to those he'd just served, and huffed twice.

"Yes," said the doctor, lifting his scotch. "To your health gentlemen."

All sipped their drinks. Pumm Pumm drained his then chewed on the cherries and orange peels. He returned the tray to the wet bar and took his dirty glass to the kitchen.

"Well damn," said Remmington. He took a second sip then held his glass at eye-level. "That monkey makes one hell of a martini!"

Worthington watched Pumm Pumm leave, then whispered. "I gotta ask, doctor, is it safe to let that thing drink?"

"It is a great deal safer than preventing him from drinking," said Schock. "And I'll thank you to refrain from calling him a 'thing' or a 'monkey.' His name is Pumm Pumm." The doctor checked his pocket watch. "And he should have dinner about ready. Shall we take our drinks to the dining room?"

"Come and race the ponies, there's a winner every time - guaranteed! I am the Track Man, and I love handing out prizes, the bigger the better!"

The Track Man, dressed in jockey togs, shouted from his game on the midway. He needed players. "One ticket buys you a seat and one of you *will* walk away with a prize! And the prizes get bigger when more people play."

"Winner every time," said Biff. "Let's get in on that."

"One ticket," said Tank. "I'd rather do the big slide again."

"C'mon, let's give it a try. It's not like we're paying for the tickets, anyway," said Chad. The boys from Mu Kau Mu took the first three seats.

"Welcome players!" said the Track Man. "Three players means a prize from the lower shelf. We need more players for bigger prizes. Come on over folks! You sir, I see you looking, have a seat there in lucky number seven. There you go, and your lady friend as well, number eight. You look like winners to me!"

The *Schock Steeplechase* was two games in one. Each numbered seat corresponded to a mechanical horse on a small track. Each seat also had its own roll-a-ball lane, where players rolled balls into target holes to move their horse along. The easier targets moved the horse one step. The harder targets moved the horse two or three.

There were seven steps in the race, and players had ten balls to get there. If a player managed to score a couple of twos or the elusive three, they took the lead and usually the win. But those higher numbers were flanked by gutters, so a miss might waste a ball.

"If we fill all the seats, we play for the top shelf!"

35

The Track Man raised a stuffed bear the size of a toddler over his head. "You've seen people carrying these around and now you know where they came from."

"Well now," said Christy Trunkett. "That is a big bear." She'd been walking the midway with Cosine, Tubes, and Sparky.

Cosine stared deeply into the roll-a-ball ramps, puzzling something out. "The singles line up," he said. "All in a row."

"Please include the group if you're going to talk out loud," said Tubes.

Cosine gave Christy a peck on the cheek. "You want one of those bears?"

"He's really cute, but he'll need his own seat if we go on any rides," said Christy.

"I'll babysit," said Sparky, who carried a good-sized bear of her own after an excellent run at the shooting gallery. "Tell us what you see, Cosine."

"There's a way to beat this. Needs a little English. Be right back." He took the last seat, which brightened the operator's mood.

"Full house, full house!" said the Track Man. "Now we've got a real race for a real prize. We are playing for the big ones on the top shelf!"

"Thanks for getting us to the top. Melvin," said Biff, calling across the other players. "Didn't know you were a fan of pedestrian sports."

"*Eques*-trian," said Cosine.

"Quiet," said Tank. "I'm trying to focus."

In Doctor Schock's lavish tent, the men laughed and told stories over plates of prime rib, scalloped potatoes, glazed carrots, and creamed spinach. Pumm

Pumm had excused himself after serving the meal. He had duties at the carnival.

Eventually, the dinner conversation turned to business.

"This carnival is a means to an end," said Schock. "A way for me to test market attractions and pricing. What I'm really after is a permanent installation. Location-based amusements are the future. Entertainment on a grand scale. People will come from all around the world to experience it."

"You mean like in California, where old Walt opened his mouse park a few years back," said Worthington.

"Heard it was a nightmare," said Barrington. "Cost overruns in the millions and a terrible opening."

"My point exactly," said Schock. "This mobile business makes a good profit. It will also help me avoid costly errors as I design my permanent installation. And I'll tell you something else - this location, Springton, interests me greatly. The speedway is already in place and drawing good crowds. You are central to many states and highways. You have good weather, too. Yes, your town of Springton is worth considering when the time comes."

The men shared happy looks around the table. "Well, Doctor," said Barrington. "We'd certainly welcome the opportunity to discuss it when the time comes."

"Very interested. Yes," said Worthington.

"That's good to hear," said Schock. "I feel comfortable enough with you gentlemen to share a secret. Would you mind?"

"We're all friends here," said Remmington. "Fire away, Doc."

"Well, here's the thing," said the doctor. "This carnival's main purpose is testing my mind tuning devices and procedures. The repetition of sound and light shaping thoughts until they align with my own."

Forks hovered over the plates as Schock's guests blinked and stared. After a pause, Remmington spoke.

"I'm sorry Doc, I don't quite follow…"

"It is my plan to bring the thoughts of everyone in the world in line with my own. To rule through technological conditioning rather than force, becoming the greatest leader in history. To create Planet Schock."

This brought a chuckle amongst the others. "Schock, you are a real showman," said Barrington. "Boys, the doctor here has cracked the secret of mind control!"

"Well, it's not mind *control*," said the doctor. "You don't need to control a mind if it agrees with you. And that's the goal. A shared point of view. *My* point of view."

The doctor twisted a dial on the side of his chair. A low, rhythmic hum rose around the table and patterned lights flashed above. His guest's expressions softened. "That's better," he said. "Now let's talk about funding and permits."

"Yes Doctor Schock," said the men. In chorus.

———

The Track Man handed pails of balls to the players. "The race starts when the bell rings and your gates drop. That's when you roll to win. If any horse crosses the finish line, the sirens go off and the race is over. When these lights spin, the winner wins." With everyone equipped, he stepped into his station and flipped two toggle switches.

The mechanical horses reared in unison and a recorded bugle played *First Call*.

"Ready," said the Track Man. "Set... GO!" He slapped a big button, the bell rang, and all ten of the gates dropped. Every player had an open lane to roll for glory.

Each of the Doltingtons rolled too hard. The balls bounced around for quite a while before they dropped. Chad scored a one, the others found the gutters.

Cosine held his ball between his palms tight. Then his left hand went back as his right hand went forward. The ball spun like a top and moved down the lane. He launched another the same way before the first one reached the holes. Then he spun two more after that.

They all banked perfectly to the four closest targets. They were spinning, so they didn't jump around. They dropped straight down the holes, earning one step each.

"Number ten is an early leader, but it's still anyone's race," said the Track Man.

"Dammit," said Biff, stuffing balls into his lane. "They bounce all around. Nothing's hitting the three."

"Quiet," said Tank.

By the time the rest of the players were lining up their third shots, Cosine had another quartet of balls spinning down his lane. They all hit their marks, and it was more than enough to send his horse across the finish line.

The siren wailed and recorded fanfare and cheering blasted from the speakers. The boys from Mu Kau Mu stormed off before the winner was announced.

The doctor spent half an hour outlining his plans. Each member of the Springton Board of Supervisors had a task to perform the next day.

"Please gentlemen, continue with your meals," said Doctor Schock. Barrington, Worthington, and Remmington resumed eating in silence. "You won't remember the specifics of this conversation, but you will certainly do what I've asked. Mr. Barrington will use his powers as mayor to get my permits pushed through the planning commission. Mr. Worthington will open a line of credit. Mr. Remmington will sponsor a live television broadcast of the Springton 50 on your local Channel 14."

The men paused with their forks elevated. "Yes Doctor Schock," they said, then put the bites in their mouths.

"Good. Very good," said the doctor. "You are under the influence of my latest brain beam. Its predecessor is still in use, and it is quite reliable. But in order for it to be effective, the subjects need to be off-balance. Exposed to adequate G-forces or an intense barrage of light and sound. Acquiring volunteers for such abuse is difficult. Acquiring involuntary subjects is illegal. But this carnival solves everything. Subjects flock here, pay money, and line up for the privilege. There are a few that suffer ill effects from the procedure, like dizziness or nausea. But they blame these symptoms on the speed of the rides or an overindulgence of cotton candy. They laugh it off and come back for more. Do you understand?"

"Yes Doctor Schock."

"Then I will continue. Recently, Pumm Pumm worked out frequency and light patterns capable of controlling subjects without jostling them about. *Passive indoctrination*, we call it. It's running now across the entire carnival. Everyone keeps spending money and having a wonderful time. In this room, with a more focused version, you are under my complete control. Best of all, we've isolated a beam we can project via a cathode ray tube."

James Remmington's brow knitted. For him, the beam's effects had slipped. "You're a fool to tell us this, Schock," he said. "We'll report you."

Schock turned the dial on the arm of his chair two clicks higher. The rhythmic hum and moving lights deepened. "Sorry, I didn't quite hear you," he said. "I believe you said something about the meal."

Remmington's gaze shifted to his plate. "I said this prime rib is remarkable."

"That's better. Are you all clear on your tasks?" asked the doctor.

"Yes Doctor Schock," said the men.

"Good," said Schock. "Mr. Remmington is brighter than he seems, gentlemen. An advanced intellect resists the beam's influence. A few moments at this level of intensity will fix the problem."

For a minute, the only sound was the machine's thrum. Then, slowly, the doctor brought the beam's power down to zero. "Thank you for coming this evening, gentlemen."

Schock led them out of the tent. "Sorry to rush you," said the doctor, "but I have been away from the carnival for hours now and I should check in with everyone."

"Not a problem, Doctor," said Worthington. "Thanks for having us. Wonderful meal, please give our compliments to Pumm Pumm."

"You can be certain I will," said the doctor.

"I'll call you once I've had a chat with the planning commission," said Barrington.

"I'll call the local TV station first thing," said Remmington.

BRET NELSON

"And I'll call Mr. Phlipworth tomorrow as soon as the bank business is taken care of," said Worthington.

"Thank you very much," said Schock. "I do appreciate it." He escorted his guests to the hidden door in the mural and out to the carnival grounds, but he did not follow them. Instead, he strolled through the backstage area beyond his marquee tent.

He walked past the generators and trucks until he came to three huge warehouse trailers. They were interconnected and climate-controlled. A sign on the side read *Employee Storage*.

The doctor pulled a key from its secret holding place in the back of his pocket watch and unlocked the door, which let out a hiss as the hermetic seal was broken. Inside, he moved among the rows of employee lockers.

Each contained an employee.

A protein slurry moved into their stomachs via tubes. Fluids moved into their arms via IVs. And each locker had a small version of Doctor Schock's brain beam, constantly pumping tasks and messages.

The doctor made his way to the control panel at the center of the lockers. He checked the readings on a number of gauges and liked what he saw. Schock lifted a handset labeled *override* and spoke into it.

"Greetings all. This is Doctor Schock," he said. His voice echoed through every locker. "You'll be glad to know our opening went well. Tomorrow, on your dayshift, you will each be filled with energy and exuding excitement. Will you be ready to serve?"

"Yes Doctor Schock," said all in perfect chorus.

"Wonderful."

5

The Lab Rats had been hard at work in the shed behind Selkirk's Gas and Tune since sunrise. A surprise was on the way for them, as Christy Trunkett had picked up a boxed dozen from the county's best shop - Dream Donut.

She got fifteen steps from the shed when the doors flew open. Clouds of orange smoke and three young scientists tumbled out.

"Hey! Good morning, Christy," said Tubes, choking.

"It's early for fireworks," said Christy. "Fourth of July is a ways out."

"I know that blue box," said Sparky between deep breaths. "You've been to Dream Donut."

"I have," said Christy. "There's enough for everyone but I'm not sure where we can eat them now. Are you guys all right?"

"We've got used to these reactions," said Cosine. "But we haven't seen orange smoke before. Hopefully it's a good sign."

"Turns out the plumes are part of the molecular bonding," said Tubes, brushing orange dust off his derby.

"I've got venting fans running in the windows," said Sparky. "The shop should be good by now."

With careful steps, they went back inside the shed. The Lab Rats washed their hands in the beat-up work sink and Christy made a clean table space for the donuts and napkins.

"We've got sodas," said Sparky. She reached for the cooler and a pop of blue jumped from her knuckle.

As he munched a maple bar, Cosine eyed the large beaker half-filled with fluid. "It's still purple, but the opacity is different this time."

Tubes pulled the goggles off his derby and snapped them over his eyes. He waved his hand behind the beaker. "Yes, it's clearer." He moved a stirring rod through the liquid then held it above and let it drip. "But look at that! Really grabs the stick."

Sparky finished off her glazed with sprinkles and pulled on her goggles. "Let's give it whirl."

As he'd done so many times before, Tubes measured out four ounces of the new formula and poured it into the prototype machine.

"Hang on a minute, don't start anything," said Cosine. He wrote what looked like a recipe in his notebook. "I've got too much margin writing and cross outs. Let me copy it over neat."

Christy finished her chocolate old fashioned. "Your writing is better than mine," she said. Then she gave him a peck on his cheek. "How do you know if it worked?"

Cosine pulled on his goggles. "Sparky's got gauges all over the prototype motor and if they read steady for long enough, then we've got our fuel additive."

"So, you'll run the race with better fuel than everyone else?" asked Christy.

"Not exactly," said Sparky. "It's not meant to power a car long term, but for a boost, to kick on an auxiliary system, it works great. And that's the Pixii's secret weapon, an extra drive system unlike anything else."

Tubes flicked the toggle switch.

"Wait a second," said Cosine. He found a set of goggles from Christy. "You should put these on, just in case."

"I should leave, just in case," said Christy. She gave Cosine a hug then spoke to the others on her way out. "I'll see you all at the fair tonight."

Once the door was closed, Tubes pulled the small cord. The machine whirred to life, hardly making a sound. "These numbers look better than ever," he said.

Cosine marked down gauge readings on his clipboard. "You're right."

———

Nigel Barrington and his son hardly ever had breakfast together. Today, the elder Barrington insisted on it, so they had eggs, toast, and fruit in the back garden. The conversation quickly turned to the temporary employment offer from Doctor Schock.

"Work at the carnival?" asked Tank. "Come on, Pop. It sounds lame."

"I am making deals with Doctor Schock," said Nigel Barrington. "Long reaching deals. Good for this family and good for this community."

"What's that got to do with me being a carny?"

"It's not carny work." Nigel sipped his coffee, lit a cigarette, and gathered his thoughts. "This is a way for you to get closer to this Schock fellow. Think about the legacy, son. Our legacy. If the doctor's plans move forward, we need to be involved. The Barrington family has been a cornerstone here for generations."

"What generations?" Tank had another slice of bacon. "You mean since Grandpa started making birdies?"

"Yes, generations. Yours is the third generation. And they aren't birdies, they are shuttlecocks. And we are expanding into tennis balls and other sport products."

"It's still a factory," said Tank. "It's dark and noisy and the people who work there hate it."

Nigel Barrington smiled. "You won't work in the factory, son. You'll be management."

"That's a nightmare, too," said Tank. "I'm terrible with numbers and I'm worse with people."

"That's not true." The elder Barrington mashed out his cigarette then smeared strawberry preserves on his toast. "You are a leader. Your friends look up to you."

"Only cause I'm bigger than they are," said Tank. He wiped his mouth and hands on his napkin then walked around the table. "Chad and Biff are jerks. They're stupid jerks, and even though they're stupid they're still smarter than me."

Nigel didn't look up from his toast. "You don't mean that."

"I'm not happy." Tank returned to his seat and looked at his father, who in turn looked at his newspaper. "I haven't been happy for as long as I can remember. I'm just this big guy who the smart kids are afraid of, and the rich kids use to get what they want. But you know what *I* want? I want to get as far away from Springton and your birdie factory as I can. Right after graduation I'm gonna join the Peace Corps and go to some jungle where money doesn't matter. Where nobody knows my family is rich. At least then

I'll know people are treating me with... treating me in a... a true way."

His father finally looked at him. "You're trying to say, 'treating you honestly,'" he said.

"See. I'm big, dumb Tank Barrington who can't even talk right."

———

Three hours later, the gauges attached to the prototype machinery still held steady.

The Formula worked.

The Lab Rats installed the extra motor and other pieces in their car. They all worked, too.

The Pixii had an edge.

"How are we ever going to test this at speed?" asked Cosine.

"The full unit going double the legal speed limit? There's really no way for that to happen until race day," said Sparky. "But I think what you really want to know is if we can win the race."

"You're right," said Cosine. "But we can't know that."

"We already know plenty," said Tubes. "Like, a cluster of four rods gets us the extra lift we're looking for."

"And thanks to your calculations, we know the Pixii will succeed if we can power six of those clusters," said Sparky.

"You're right," said Cosine. "And this fuel additive is efficient and powerful enough to run the extra motor at the right RPM. That was the last piece."

"The math and the components work," said Tubes. "Sparky's been driving cars since she was ten years old, she's got it handled."

"Sure do," said Sparky. She held up a small box

47

and rocked it back and forth. "Even got these boss driving gloves."

"So cool," said Cosine. "Yesterday I measured the guardrails at the speedway again, and we're good there. You guys are right. We are as ready as we can be. We'll learn the rest during the race."

"Will we win? Maybe," said Sparky. "But we're up against a Bendix Electrojector system. Something we weren't expecting."

"But remember, there will be a Doltington controlling it," said Cosine. "That's in our favor."

"Even if we don't come in first," said Tubes. "We will certainly prove out this new fuel additive and our new drive systems. At the same time, we'll earn enough credits to graduate. Those are wins."

"Big wins," said Cosine. "Let's get the Pixii on the flatbed. It's ready."

———

At 11:00am, the boys from Mu Kau Mu showed up at the gate. Mr. Phlipworth was waiting for them.

"Good morning, gentlemen," he said, shaking hands all around. "You must be Tank Barrington. And you are Biff Worthington, I'd wager. And you sir, must be Chad. Spitting image of your father with that bold Remmington chin."

"Yeah," said Chad. "Didn't catch your name."

"I am Mr. Phlipworth. Sheldon Phlipworth. I manage things for Doctor Schock."

"That's swell, Mr. Phlipworth," said Chad. "My old man said you had some kinda jobs available. Good pay for a couple of hours. Is that right?"

"Doctor Schock has a job offer, yes," said Phlipworth. "You'll be paid well for your time, only a few hours each day."

"What kind of work is this?" asked Tank. "All these carnival jobs look like knuckle-busters."

"Yeah," said Chad. "I don't want to go home smelling like corn dogs."

"We aren't fans of annual labor," said Biff.

That gave Phlipworth a pause. "I believe you mean *manual* labor, Mr. Worthington. In any case, it won't be an issue. You see, the doctor is developing new screens for television viewing, and he needs people to test them. To make sure the picture and sound remain clear over time. The job is watching TV."

Phlipworth led the boys through the mural's secret door and into the backstage area of the carnival. "Follow me, gentlemen," he said. Their destination was a row of large trailers near the doctor's tent. "These house our Research and Development projects. Come along, let's go inside."

Inside was a single room. Bare, except for three large chairs facing an enormous console television set.

"This is where we work?" said Tank.

"What gives?" asked Biff.

"Please, sit in those chairs," said Phlipworth. The boys did so. "There is a lever on the side, and if you pull it..."

"Whoa," said Chad. "Recliners! Sweet!"

"Yes. Very sweet," said Phlipworth. "Now, all you have to do is watch television." He checked the wires leading into the back of the set, then powered it on. A test pattern came into focus.

"That's a really big screen," said Tank.

"It is indeed," said Phlipworth. "As I said, it is a prototype for use in a future attraction. Watch any channel you like. After three hours, you'll answer some questions about the video and sound quality. That's the whole job."

49

"We get paid to watch a giant TV," said Biff. "That's like a dream."

"Each of you will receive a $50 bill at the end of the day's session," said Phlipworth. He handed Chad a bulky remote control.

"Will you look at that," said Chad. "We even get a clicker." He pressed a button, the test pattern vanished, and Bill Cullen filled the screen.

"Hey! *The Price is Right!*" said Tank. "I'm pretty good at this."

"Man, this is living," said Biff, settling in his chair.

"Yes it is," said Phlipworth. "There are coolers between the chairs with sodas if you'd like one. I have duties elsewhere, so I'll leave you to it. See you in a few hours." The boys said their goodbyes as Phlipworth left and closed the door behind him.

"Sodas, too," said Chad. "That Doc Schock thinks of everything."

From a hidden room behind the vast television set, Doctor Schock replied unheard. "Indeed, Mr. Remmington, I have thought of everything." He sat at a control console with closed-circuit views of each of his three subjects. The lever on the console had eight numbered settings. "Let's see how you dimwits handle strength two."

He pulled the lever into the second slot. Each of boys sat upright, wide-eyed. Schock waited a few minutes, and aside from blinks, swallows, and other autonomic responses, they remained resolutely still.

"Likely the quietest they've been in years," said the doctor. He spoke into a microphone on the console and his voice came over the television's speaker "This is Doctor Schock. Look to your right."

The boys did so.

"Look back to the television," said the doctor. Again, they did so. The doctor switched the microphone off. "So far so good. Television really is the future. It will unite nations, unite the world."

The doctor donned a dome-shaped helmet covered with transistors and coils. It was hard-wired into the console at a junction labeled *Direct Control*. "Let's give the new system a whirl."

Schock clicked three buttons, and the helmet lit up. He shuddered for a moment, then smiled.

And concentrated.

And concentrated more.

"Yes Doctor Schock," said the boys watching the television. "We hear and obey."

———

Walking the carnival grounds, seeing the people soon to be under the doctor's complete control, Phlipworth often wondered if his thoughts were his own. Schock said an awareness of the brain beams made one immune to their influence, yet doubts remained.

Then again, if his mind was being controlled by the doctor, could he have doubts? Probably not.

He believed in the work the Doctor was doing. He looked forward to the world they were building. These feelings weren't the effect of any brain beam. He felt a purity of purpose and wonder.

Phlipworth stopped at the main ticket booth to make sure the girl running it had everything she needed. She smiled at him and the customers, a model employee. The ticket sheets and booklets were well organized, each tiled out in its proper row. The maps of the carnival and the guides to the midway games were clean and tidy in their boxes.

However, he found trouble in the till. Several nickels had found their way into the section of the tray reserved for the quarters. And the rolled coins were all in a stack, not lined up by denomination.

Shoddy. Disordered. He'd demonstrated how to organize the cash drawer, yet here the operator had decided to show some kind of personal flair. Worse yet, perhaps they didn't even care.

Phlipworth made a note in his report to the doctor. Operator 616 will need a more intense setting on the brain beam the next time she's in storage.

———

Schock pulled the helmet off his head, carefully laid it on its stand, and spent a moment congratulating himself. The equipment worked flawlessly. Doctor Schock's instructions, his very will moved along the cathode ray tubes and into the minds of the youths seated in front of the television set.

"The next step will take place during your Springton 50 auto race," he said aloud, gazing at the blank faces of the Doltingtons on his closed-circuit screens. "During the live broadcast, my Ultimate Brain Beam shall ride along the signal. A stowaway. And the cathode ray tubes in the television receivers will carry my commands into thousands of homes, controlling thousands of minds at once. In time I shall sponsor a national ad campaign during prime-time television. Then an international campaign."

The doctor looked skyward. "Tomorrow, this town will host the arrival of Planet Schock."

The doctor made a few adjustments to the controls to keep the boys mollified in their recliners, then he moved to a room behind the control center. A brainstorming and study area with a few chairs around a table and a large chalkboard on the wall.

He'd scratched a few notes on the chalkboard

when it occurred to him he wasn't meant to be alone. "Odd," he said, checking his pocket watch.

Intense and focused, Pumm Pumm came through the door with an armload of large-format documents.

"There you are," said Schock. "I was worried. Not like you to be late." The gorilla tossed the papers on the table and plopped into a seat.

"You've reviewed the plans for our permanent installation, I see. These are reliant on getting the college in line with our goals. We need their land. Hopefully Dean Trunkett won't be a problem. He refuses to attend the carnival. Spends all his time at the college's recruitment booth at the fair. Agriculture school, or at least it was for decades. Leaning hard into the sciences of late. Yes, good group for us to be affiliated with, don't you think?"

Pumm Pumm stared at Schock. Most of the time, the doctor knew what was on the gorilla's mind, but at this moment his expression was inscrutable.

Even for an ape.

"What troubles you?" asked the doctor. "Is it those fools in the other room? They will be fine unattended for at least another hour."

Massive hands dug through the pile of papers. Pumm Pumm tugged the proposed map of the park out of the pile and shoved the page in front of the doctor. He thumped the paper emphatically with his great forefinger.

A large section of the map was labeled *zoo*. The margin notes detailed the planned exhibits there, including a monkey house.

After all they'd been through together, the ape understood more about Doctor Eduard Schock than anyone else, even more than Phlipworth. He understood the doctor had no moral compass. His sole purpose was to unite the human race under his will.

But this idea of imprisoning wild animals in tiny, counterfeit versions of their actual homelands. The thought of rude people staring at them as their horrible children pelted them with popcorn. It was more than the ape could stand.

A betrayal beyond his ability to stomach.

"Oh, I see the problem," said Schock, peering at the map. "Yes, part of the complex must be dedicated to animals. Can't be helped."

The doctor pulled a document from the stack titled *Competitor Analysis* and handed it to Pumm Pumm. "There, in the second column, you'll see there's a very popular zoo a short drive away from here. Their most popular exhibit is the primates display. If we don't want to lose customers to them, we will need to have a zoo of our own."

Pumm Pumm shook his head.

"Please, don't take it personally," said Schock. "With your input on their care and environments, I'm certain they will be very happy with us." The doctor stood and moved toward the door. "I'm needed elsewhere. Can you keep an eye on the boys watching television until Phlipworth arrives? He should be here in two hours."

The ape nodded, and Schock left. In that moment, things became clear to Pumm Pumm. The doctor was going to build a zoo, regardless of anyone else's feelings on the matter. And though Schock called him *old friend*, they were anything but.

Yes, it was clear to him now. The time had come for Pumm Pumm to execute *his own* plans.

He moved into the control room and studied the boys from Mu Kau Mu on the hidden camera screens. Then he opened a panel on the side of the console and changed the configuration of four components.

Next, Pumm Pumm took a transistor module of

his own design from his shirt pocket and swapped it with a similar module on Schock's helmet. He took a seat behind the console and placed the helmet firmly on his head.

The gorilla clicked five buttons on the panel and the helmet lit up. He moved the lever into the fifth position, and watched as the three youths went dull-eyed in their chairs.

Pumm Pumm had made his own refinements to this version of the brain beam. It allowed him to read the minds in the other room as well as control them. It allowed him to sweep their brains and learn about humans.

Learn how to be one.

And in this group of young people, he found a kindred spirit, the one they called Tank. Frustrated with his place and wanting something different. Trapped with no real hope of escape.

The ape turned knobs and moved sliders, focusing the beam solely on the mind of Tank Barrington. A connection formed.

Tank saw the gorilla's eyes on the television screen. And in his head, he heard a rumbling baritone voice.

"Hello," it said. "I have a proposition."

———

James Remmington spoke calmly into the phone. His office at Remmington Luxury Motors had four sales-people lined up outside. They each had customers ready to sign, but they needed the boss's signature on the paperwork.

He ignored them. He was working a larger deal for Doctor Schock. "They need a check today," said Remmington.

Robert Worthington was on the other end of the call at his bank. "The money dropped into the account this morning," he said. "I'll bring them the check myself. Have it there in an hour."

"That's great," said Remmington. "The Springton 50 broadcast live on Channel 14! Sponsored by my dealerships. Cameras will get set up first thing in the morning. We're on the air for the whole thing."

"Wonderful. Did they get their sports guy to host?"

"Yup. Paid another thousand to get Chip Stevens on the mic."

"It's costing us a fortune," said Worthington. "But I'm so happy about it."

"Me too," said Remmington. "Why does this feel so right?"

———

The communication between Tank and Pumm Pumm was beyond speech. Their minds were linked as one, so ideas and exchanges occurred without conversation. Occurred instantly. And they both loved the plan.

Each would get exactly what they had been wishing for. Together they took deep breaths, and Pumm Pumm engaged a secret lever on the control panel. The brain beam connecting the human and the ape pulsed and pulled as the machinery wailed.

Tank closed his eyes. There was a change in the temperature of the room. He felt a jerk from head to toe, something like a sneeze. Then the machinery grew quiet.

He heard the baritone voice in his head again. "You can open your eyes now," it said.

Tank's view was blurred for a moment, then came

into sharper focus than he had ever experienced. He found himself in a different room, in a different chair looking over a control panel covered with levers, buttons, and dials. No idea how any of it worked. Three screens across the top of the panel carried images of himself, Chad, and Biff in the recliners.

He felt well. Strong, but not unusual. He wondered if the transfer had even happened.

When he looked down at his massive gorilla hands, he knew it had.

The voice continued. "This link will tie our minds so long as we remain here, but now that the mind-swap has taken place, our communication will be more like a conversation."

"But still in our heads, right?" asked Tank, in his new, simian head. "I'm a gorilla now, but in my mind I still sound like me. It's confusing."

"No one else can hear us. We are linked telepathically."

"Do Biff or Chad know about this?"

"Your friends are still unaware of their surroundings."

"They're *your* friends now. You're Tank Barrington. And I'm Pumm Pumm. Hey, is Pumm Pumm my real name?"

"Gorillas don't use names. In the wild, communication is immediate, and you can see who you are talking to. Names are unnecessary. But humans will call you Pumm Pumm. Is 'Tank' my real name?"

"It's Bertram, after your grandfather."

"I'll stick with 'Tank.'" He rose from the recliner and took a few steps on his new, human legs. Longer than he was used to, yet weaker. He jogged in place. "It's going to take a few minutes for us to get in tune with our new physiologies. Things we did with little thought should be available immediately, albeit in a limited capacity. For instance, it will take time for me to communicate fully, but a limited vocabulary will be accessible right away. You will be able to climb intuitively, but don't try swinging until a few days have passed."

"Got it." Pumm Pumm, who used to be Tank, thought for a moment. "Here's something weird... I know a lot about the carnival. Has to be from you, right? Guess it stayed behind from the transfer."

"Yes, and I know a great deal about the Barrington family, and your father's business dealings."

"Your father, now."

"Yes. My father. So much to keep track of. For a time, the hardest part will be remembering what we can no longer do. I won't be as strong as I once was. You will not be able to speak."

There was a silence for a few minutes, each experiencing new sensations.

The young man finally spoke out loud. "Hey," he said.

The gorilla nodded. Tank's voice was strong.

Tank resumed telepathic communication "Not bad, I'll need to keep at it. We should break this connection and join the rest of the world."

"This is gonna be weird."

"And wonderful. There is a large lever in the center of the console. Slowly, bring it to level two. Once it's there, I'll join you in the control room and put things back the way they were. We can also take the helmet off your head."

"Helmet?" He didn't even know he was wearing it.

Officials at the Speedway had their hands full checking in all the cars for the Springton 50. Despite the entrants receiving a staggered schedule for arrival, all twenty of them got there at more or less the same time. Some arrived on flatbeds, others drove in on their own power with their engines making enough noise to drown out the carnival.

The Dodge D-500 Remmington Racer came through the gates with its horn blaring. Chad Remmington was behind the wheel with his father in the passenger seat. They were waved into their parking slot by a harried man with a clipboard.

"Please, refrain from blowing that horn," he said.

Chad continued pressing the bar on the steering wheel and hollering to Biff Worthington. "Biff! Get over here and look at this beast!"

After a few more honks, Biff finally noticed the car and charged over. His father, Robert Worthington, and Nigel Barrington approached at a more reasonable pace. Biff and Chad opened the hood and stared at the D-500's space-age engine, complete with a Bendix Electrojector.

The elder Remmington filled out forms for the harried man with the clipboard. Nigel Barrington tapped the Remmington Motors logo painted on the car's door. "Jimmy," he said, "I never want to hear you complain about me promoting my factory again."

Remmington filled in the last space on the last form and signed it. "Looks good, doesn't it? All shiny and gold."

"Are you the driver, sir?" asked the man with the clipboard.

"My son is the driver."

"He needs to sign here."

"Chad, get your nose out of that engine and get over here," said Remmington.

"Where the hell is Tank?" asked Chad, signing the form.

"Yes," said Robert Worthington, "Where's your boy, Nigel?"

"Said he'd be here," said Biff. "He must have got diffracted by something at the carnival."

"*Dis*-stracted," said Barrington.

There was a murmur through the speedway as a gorilla made his way through the crowd. Alongside walked Tank Barrington. They joined the others at the Remmington Racer.

"Well, it's about time," said Chad.

"Hello Tank," said James Remmington.

Pumm Pumm tried to say "hi," but no words came out. Tank nudged him and the ape covered his mouth with one hand.

"Hey," said Tank, waving to the group.

"And hello Pumm Pumm," said Barrington, tossing his cigarette away. "Hope my boy here isn't causing you any grief."

Pumm Pumm shook his head and gave Tank a slap on the back. It nearly knocked him over. Tank recovered quickly and smiled an awkward smile. His father leaned in and whispered in his ear.

"Glad to see you've made a friend in the organization. Well done, boy."

"Hey," said Tank.

"This car is so boss," said Biff. "This is totally gonna blow the egghead car off the road!" All eyes moved to the parking slot five spaces away, where the Lab Rats were easing the Pixii off the flatbed from Selkirk's Gas and Tune

"What a heap," said James Remmington. "I'll be surprised if it rolls off the flatbed in one piece."

That got laughs from everyone, especially Tank. And his laughter was especially loud.

"For the love of Mike, it wasn't that funny," said Chad.

Tank's face went straight. "Hey," he said.

———

The Pixii not only made it off the flatbed in one piece, but it also ran its mandatory two laps at a sustained speed of 60 MPH without incident, as did the Remmington Racer.

Two cars didn't last the two laps and were disqualified, which meant there would be eighteen entrants when the race started at 10am the next morning.

The Springton Board of Supervisors left the Speedway to pay a visit to Dean Trunkett at the fair. The dean had been spending most of his time at the Springton College Recruiting Booth there.

On the advice of his father, Chad went straight home to get plenty of rest, as he'd be the driver for the D-500. Biff, who always mirrored Chad, decided to head home as well.

This obedient behavior had been implanted by Doctor Schock.

Tank stayed behind to spend time with his new friend Pumm Pumm.

The Lab Rats had been doing math, engineering, and chemistry most of the day and needed to blow off some steam. Christy Trunkett joined them, and they spent the evening wandering around the carnival.

After their third consecutive run on the *Schocking Speedster*, Christy and the Lab Rats didn't get back in line for a fourth.

"That thing is a blast," said Christy. "But I think I've had enough coasters for now."

"I'm out of tickets anyway," said Tubes. "And I'm beat. Time for me to head home."

"I didn't want to be the first to conk out," said Sparky. "Thanks for being feeble."

Tubes reached out with shaky hands and spoke in a slow, hoarse whisper. "What's that you say, youngster?"

"Let's get you out of here, Gramps," said Sparky. She took his arm for support and a blue glint popped from her fingers.

"Gah!" croaked Tubes. "Youth of today is dangerous!"

"Electricity is in my blood," said Sparky.

"We've got enough tickets for one more ride," said Christy. "See you guys tomorrow."

———

In the broadcast booth at the Speedway, the Springton Board of Supervisors listened attentively as Doctor Schock held court.

"To think, from this booth tomorrow your own local celebrity Chip Stevens will thrill all those watching Channel 14 with a live broadcast of the Springton 50!"

"We couldn't be happier," said the men.

The doctor looked past the speedway to the light of the carnival. "The microwave relay dish high atop this booth has a direct line of sight to my own dish atop the control tower at the carnival. While their broadcast is running, I'll be hiding in the air chain, creating a pathway between everyone's television set and my Ultimate Brain Beam! Electron by electron, the picture tube in each home will carry my commands and begin our march towards history. Tomorrow morning, we welcome thousands of new citizens to Planet Schock!"

"We couldn't be happier," said the men.

"Go home, gentlemen. I'll forgive your repeated failures to convince the dean to help us. Perhaps we can find another way."

———

Cosine and Christy had been debating about their last ride for some time. She wanted to explore the spook house. Cosine wanted to do anything else.

"Of course I don't think there are ghosts in there," said Cosine. "If we were going to discover evidence of the afterlife, it wouldn't be at this carnival."

"I still say you're chicken," said Christy. She put her arms around his shoulders and kissed his cheek. "You'll be okay. I'll hold your hand the whole time."

"I am chicken – of strobe lights," said Cosine. "Those stuttering flashes give me the worst headaches. It can mess me up for days."

Christy stepped away from him and crossed her arms in a mock pout. "If you won't go on *Schock's Haunted Castle* with me, I'll go by myself."

"Okay, I'll go," said Cosine. "But if there's lights jumping around, I'm putting my head down. But it's not because I'm scared."

She took his hand and pulled him along. "Onward brave knight, to yonder haunted castle!"

In the control tower, Doctor Schock arrived to double check the connections on his microwave relay dish. "All is well," he said. "Tomorrow will be wonderful."

Phlipworth dialed through the hidden camera views around the carnival. "Doctor, have you seen Pumm Pumm? Can't find him anywhere."

"He's been spending a great deal of time with one of those fools from the fraternity. Tank, I think he's called."

"Oh yes, I saw them earlier," said Phlipworth. "Tank Barrington. The beams have clearly captured his will. Good for Pumm Pumm to have an extra set of hands, I suppose."

"He can do as he likes," said Schock. "I've upset him with the inclusion of a zoo at the new park. If spending time with this person helps his feelings heal, that's wonderful."

Phlipworth paused a moment, then focused the viewer on Christy Trunkett.

"Excuse me, Doctor," he said. "This young lady is on our watchlist."

Schock joined him. "Tell me about her."

"She is Christine Trunkett, the daughter of Eugene Trunkett who is Dean of Springton College." Phlipworth handed a notecard to Doctor Schock. "Her mother, Lydia Trunkett died in a car accident when Christine was six years old."

"And the young man with her?"

"Melvin Carstairs. Senior at Springton College," said Phlipworth, passing another notecard. "Outstanding student. Excels in mathematics."

"We have little need of an accountant," said the doctor. "However, the girl may prove useful if she has any influence over her father. Earlier, the board of supervisors failed to convince him to help us."

"They are heading to the castle," said Phlipworth. "Shall I join them?"

"Yes, please do. And let me know as soon as she's in range."

———

Schock's Haunted Castle sported a sheet metal facade painted to look like a crumbling old palace with all sorts of ghosts and monsters and nasties staring out the windows and flying circles around the parapets.

Behind the facade, a simple, enclosed structure housed the attraction. Up to four riders sat in a phony casket and got pulled along a track by a chain. The technology wasn't sophisticated, but the props in this spook house set it apart from others. Each area was dressed like a Hollywood monster movie set. Guests moved through a mad scientist's lab, a ghastly kitchen, a sinister dining hall, and an eerie looking graveyard.

The cart/casket tripped switches that made dummies bounce on springs and swoop on wires. These figures sported enough silly gore to earn an honest shriek, then pay the shriek off with a laugh.

Wind cannons blasted and dangling cloth ribbons brushed over the guests as creepy sound effects and music blared from hidden speakers.

Cosine and Christy progressed through the queue. Phlipworth arrived and positioned himself in the loading area. Recalling his barker days, he teased the people waiting to be next. "Earlier two riders didn't make it out," he said in his deepest, spookiest voice. "You'll find them inside, haunting the graveyard… forever!"

With his best smile, he moved among those nearest the front and asked who wanted to ride in a group and how many there were and made sure everyone had their tickets ready.

And because of Phlipworth's subtle shifts in the line, Cosine and Christy found themselves seated in a casket alone.

"Next group has four and they want to ride together," said Phlipworth. "Looks like you lovebirds have this cart to yourselves." He collected their tickets and pulled the safety bar across their laps.

"Hear that, Cosine? All alone in a casket built for two."

"Yeah," said Cosine, still worried about the strobe lights. "It's like a dream."

They snuggled up close. The double doors, painted to look like a drawbridge, swung open. The screams of anguished spirits greeted them as their casket moved inside.

Phlipworth spoke into a handset at the ride operator's station. "The dean's daughter is in the castle," he said.

In the control tower, Schock hovered over the main console. "Excellent," he said. "Thank you Phlipworth." The doctor turned the tuning knobs, and the hidden camera feed showed Christy Trunkett and Cosine Carstairs moving through the mad scientist's lab within *Schock's Haunted Castle*.

———

"This stuff looks really good," said Cosine.

"Yeah," said Christy. "It's like riding through a movie."

Their casket stopped in front of a crude operating table with a creature strapped to it. The table flipped upright suddenly, standing the creature in front of them.

They both jumped. "Got you," said Christy.

"Got us both," said Cosine. Sparks flew around the creature's head. "Uh oh. Here come the strobes."

He was right. The speakers blared music and a scratchy voice screaming about "lightning and reanimation." The room lit up with flashes and stuttering spotlights. Cosine ducked his head into Christy's shoulder. She locked her eyes on the pulsing bulbs.

Because they carried the brain beam.

And threaded inside the sound effects, she heard a voice speaking only to her.

In the tower, Schock spoke into a small microphone. "Christine Trunkett, this is Doctor Schock. You are in my control, nod if you understand."

She nodded.

"You will convince your father to speak with me. To seek me out. To listen to my proposal. Nod if you understand."

She nodded again.

"Nothing is more important. You must make your father listen. Do as I command." With that, the doctor took the brain beam slowly off line.

Christy Trunkett whispered, "Yes Doctor Schock."

Cosine took a peek with one eye and saw the lights had stopped thrashing. Their casket moved out of the lab and into the nightmare kitchen. "Whew," he said. "All clear. What were you saying?"

"Nothing, Melvin. Just remembered something I've got to tell my Dad."

Eugene Trunkett and his daughter had breakfast together most every morning. The kitchen table had the usual eggs, toast, and fruit cocktail.

"You should think about it Dad," said Christy. "This Schock fellow has a lot going on. There's a lot of science and engineering at the carnival. You should spend some time with him before they pack up and leave."

"I'll tell you what I told those blowhards on the Board of Supervisors yesterday," said Trunkett. "All my time during this fair is scheduled out. I'm meeting with incoming students and their parents. When that's not happening, I'm meeting with patrons and scholarship sponsors and grant providers. If this Schock fellow wants to become one of those, he can call the office and get on the schedule."

This wasn't working. Christy felt compelled to get her father closer to the carnival if nothing else.

"Can you at least come with me to the race today?" she asked. "Watch Sparky drive the car the gang has been working on?"

"That's right," said the dean. "Terklehopper mentioned that. And you'll be there with your young man Carstairs, won't you?"

"As close as they'll let me," she said. "Melvin will be down on the field, and I don't think I can be down there."

"Melvin?" said the dean. "Thought you called him 'Cosine.'"

———

For fifteen minutes, Phlipworth waited by the main ticket booth for Pumm Pumm. His impatience grew, and finally he left their appointed place to go and look for the ape. "Not like him to be tardy," said Phlipworth aloud.

He found Pumm Pumm in the unlikeliest of places. His bunk. The gorilla was the earliest riser Phlipworth had ever met, and there he was asleep.

Phlipworth shook him. "What's the matter with you? You've spent the entire morning in bed."

The gorilla's eyes opened, and he sat up, surprised.

"Yes, sleepyhead. It's late," said Phlipworth. He opened the drapes with a flourish. "Race starts in two hours, and you are needed."

The ape was busy looking at his right hand, moving his fingers in slow twiddles. His other hand explored an area of his back he could never reach in his old body.

"Stop that scratching," snapped Phlipworth. "That Tank Barrington fellow is clearly a bad influence. Now get up and get dressed, there's much to do."

Pumm Pumm stared at him, then found his clipboard with the day's tasks. He waved it over his head, nodding.

Phlipworth left saying, "I'll see you at the main booth in ten minutes. Ten!"

With the rude man gone, Pumm Pumm spent a few moments leaping around the room, enjoying his newfound strength and senses.

———

The grandstands at the Springton Speedway were full. Still more people crowded around the fence. The cameras for Channel 14 stood at key points around the track and Chip Stevens was all set up in the booth for the broadcast.

Hundreds of families didn't want to fight the crowds and instead tuned their television sets to Channel 14. And at 9:45, Chip Stevens flashed his winning smile and talked to each and every one of them.

"Good morning everyone, Chip Stevens here, from Channel 14's *Sports With Stevens!* And what a beautiful day it is here at the Springton Speedway for the tenth annual Springton 50! Thanks to our wonderful sponsor, Remmington Motors, you'll see every minute of this exciting, high-speed, 50-mile race!"

Across the fairgrounds, above the control tower at Doctor Schock's Carnival, an innocent looking microwave dished powered on. Directly beneath, in the control booth, Phlipworth checked the numbers and spoke into a handset.

"This signal is solid, Doctor Schock," said Phlipworth. "You are in. If you think it, they will know it. All will obey you."

Schock sat in his control chair in the Research and Development trailer with the Ultimate Brain Beam Helmet strapped to his head. He spoke to Phlipworth via the console's handset. "Yes," he said. "Yes. I can feel it. Already I feel my thoughts reaching out. When we are nearer the end of the race, I'll make my big push. We will capture the largest, most engaged audience."

"Yes, Doctor Schock," said Phlipworth. "Signing off."

All eighteen cars were prepped and ready on the starting line, engines revving and knuckles on steering wheels. "Isn't it exciting?" asked Christy Trunkett, seated with her father in the grandstands. She had convinced the dean to attend.

"Yes," he said. "Exciting and *loud*. Which one belongs to Carstairs and his bunch?"

She scanned the cars. "There, third from the left, the brown one."

"Oof," said the dean. "I think I drove one of those to my first date with your mother."

"Don't worry, Dad. They've made a lot of improvements."

Sparky Selkirk had set up a two-way radio in the car, so she'd be able to communicate with Tubes and Cosine all through the race. Waiting for the flag, she spoke into her transceiver. "Check check," she said. "We're starting soon. Is this signal clear?"

Cosine squeezed the talk button on the handset where he and Tubes were stationed in the field. "Loud and clear," he said. "How are we coming through?"

"Perfect," said Sparky.

The station for the Remmington Racer team was about ten yards from Tubes and Cosine. They didn't have a radio or even chairs. Biff and Tank stood there waiting. If they wanted to tell Chad something, they had to shout and hope for the best. Chad didn't hear them over the rock station he'd found on the radio. Whenever he saw them with their hands cupped around their mouths, he nodded and gave them a thumbs up anyway.

And in the roped off, VIP section of the grandstands, Nigel Barrington, James Remmington, and Robert Worthington waited impatiently for the race to begin. "I'm so excited," said Barrington. "We've spent so much money, and I'm very happy!"

"Yes, very happy," said Remmington and Worthington.

Chip Stevens got the nod from his director. "All right everyone," he said, "as you can see, Walter Cushfield, the winner of the first Springton 50 race in 1949 is climbing to the top of the risers at the starting line with the green flag in his hand. The engines are revving, and the crowd is going mad."

Cushfield took his position and held up the flag. The local papers popped off dozens of pictures. Then, he nodded to the drivers and waved the green flag with a well-practiced flourish.

"There's the start!" said Stevens. "The Springton 50 has begun!"

In households all over Springton, more and more people gathered in front of their television sets. They didn't speak. Their expressions were blank. Schock's beam was seeping into their minds.

At the first turn on the first lap, three different cars miscalculated their speed and spun into the infield. As each driver stepped from their vehicle unharmed, the crowd cheered. "Holy Moly," said Stevens. "That leaves fifteen cars, and we haven't even finished a lap. Coming out of the first turn, it's the Remmington Racer in the lead. But there's twenty-five laps in this race, so they'll really have to work to hang on to that position."

Sparky Selkirk had no trouble on the turns. She'd upgraded the suspension on the Pixii herself and it hung on fine while banking. Going into the third lap, she spoke to her team.

"Kinda crowded here, guys," she said. Though she was in a respectable seventh place, she was boxed in. And these were amateur drivers jockeying for position.

"You're right," said Tubes, looking through his binoculars. "Maybe drop back a few and get out of the crowd. Let them thin out, then you can move up later with the Max-drive."

So it went for the next fifteen laps. Car after car failed to negotiate the turns and spun out. The Remmington Racer held the lead, thanks more to its Electrojector than to Chad Remmington's driving.

The time had come. From his control console, Doctor Schock moved the main lever to the eighth position, its maximum. His helmet pulsed and he gripped the arms of his command chair.

His thoughts flowed outward to everyone watching in Springton.

And everyone in front of a television set took a simultaneous breath.

"Yes, Doctor Schock," they said.

———

No one at the Speedway was aware of the birth of Planet Schock. They were watching the actual event, not the broadcast.

Chad Remmington was bored. He was a full lap ahead of his nearest competitor, a local hot rodder who worked at Freeman's Garage in the next town.

Three laps had passed without a single car spinning out. Seven cars left in the race. "Looks like we've eliminated the lousier drivers," said Sparky. "Feels like it's time, eh?"

"Yes," said Cosine. "Four laps to go and the other cars are all single file."

"We're more than a lap behind," said Tubes. "Fire up the Max-drive, Sparky!"

She flipped the red toggle by the steering wheel and a small ready-light glowed. "Running it up now," she said, and yanked a handle they'd added to the dash.

The Max-drive kicked on, just as it did on the table in their workshop. Its reservoir was filled with their experimental fuel formulation, much more than four ounces. It spun with remarkable power. But it wasn't part of the Pixii's engine.

All its energy moved through a series of gears that cranked a dynamo under the back seat. The dynamo produced enough electricity to light half the state. Sparky giggled as she felt her hair floating in the static. She eyed one of the gauges she'd installed on the dash as its needle snapped to the right.

"The meter is at the peak," she said. "Here goes." She grabbed the lever next to the gearshift.

"See you in the winner's circle," said Tubes. He and Cosine shook hands for luck. A small blue flash passed between them.

"Ouch," said Cosine. "I think we need better shielding next time."

Sparky twisted the lever and pulled it back, switching the dynamo's full energy output to an array of super-charged electro-magnetic rods they'd installed under the car. Their clusters of alternating poles created a cushion of energy that lifted the Pixii right off the track.

Power cycled across the energy cushion. The Pixii hovered and shot forward, unencumbered by gravity or friction. Baffles controlled by the steering wheel allowed navigation to the left or right.

On the initial kick, the Pixii jumped from 70 MPH to 150 MPH.

"Holy Moly," said Chip Stevens. "Look at the Pixii! Tell you what, I believe in magic now!" His director was talking with the sound technician. Stevens covered his mic. "Is everything all right, Tony?"

"Some kind of interference, but it's okay. We're good."

Cosine tried to keep the Pixii in his binocular's field of view, but it was difficult with all the speed. "How's the fuel consumption?" he asked.

"Well within limits," said Sparky. "Dynamo is holding strong and steady. Ride is smooth. Looks like we can keep this up for hours."

"First turn's coming," said Tubes. "That may cut our run short."

"The calculations are right," said Cosine. "This is going to work."

The Pixii barreled straight for the guardrail. Sparky twisted a joystick, sending a portion of the magnetic force outside the gravity cushion. She used the steel guardrail's magnetic attraction to pull into and out of the bank at high speed. She blasted through the turn and passed all the competing cars on the next straightaway.

She overtook the Remmington Racer easily, because it wasn't moving at all.

The initial massive rush of power to the electromagnetic rod clusters had an unexpected side effect. An energy wave pulsed outward in all directions.

The computer inside the Doltington's Remmington Racer erupted in sparks and broke into three pieces. The Electrojector had become a chunk of useless plastic and metal. The car lost its space-age brain and became dumber than the idiot behind the wheel. It rolled to a stop near the infield, where Chad kept trying to start the dead thing while Biff stood next to the car and yelled at him. Tank laughed his loud, off-putting laugh.

But more importantly, the computer chips and transistor technology clustered in Doctor Schock's Ultimate Brain Beam Helmet went absolutely haywire. The device sent a series of jumbled commands to itself and created a feedback loop. Smoke poured from the sputtering dome as the brain beam shut down.

All over the carnival, in the employee lockers, and on every television set, the beam shut down.

The doctor's signals spun back into his own head over and over, nearly at the speed of light. His mind had became so overloaded with energy and errors that he experienced a level of pain heretofore unknown to anyone.

Schock's left eye lolled independent of the right one as he pawed at the control levers, knowing he had to stop this, but not knowing how.

He didn't know anything anymore.

Not even his own identity. He only knew pain.

After four minutes in this hell, he collapsed in the command chair. He didn't have the ability to maintain his respiratory functions. His lungs and heart stopped.

His superior mind didn't help him. He found his place in history, just another dead man.

Everyone under Schock's influence had their free will returned, strong as it had ever been. People at the carnival, in front of television sets, and even in their employee lockers lost their connection to the doctor.

And long after the Lab Rats had collected their trophy and oversized cardboard check, Robert Worthington, Nigel Barrington, and James Remmington remained in their seats with the slack-jawed realization of all they had done over the past few days.

"Oh my word," said Worthington. "We're ruined."

The carnival shut down in pieces as the ride operators came to their senses. The police arrived quickly and discovered the horrors behind the secret door in the mural, including the twisted corpse of Doctor Eduard Schock.

Over the weeks that followed, the FBI and investigators from every state arrived to quantify Schock's wrongdoings. They were voluminous, but with the complete destruction of every part of his Ultimate Brain Beam, his greatest crime would remain undiscovered forever.

7

Melvin Carstairs, Josephine Selkirk, and Stanley Terklehopper all graduated from Springton College at the top of their class. The Pixii, their senior project, got high marks and a lot of attention from entities outside the school.

Of course, the damage caused by the magnetic shockwave (later called an EMP) made putting these engines into consumer automobiles a terrible idea. But a sealed system, say for a train, would be a wonderful application of the technology. And many companies made many offers for each of the Lab Rats to come and work for them.

Cosine and Christy opted to stay in Springton for a time. He taught math at the college and waited a year for her to graduate, then they both left to design systems at Bell Labs in New Jersey.

Sparky Selkirk got scooped up by the Jet Propulsion Laboratory in sunny California. Up the coast, Tubes Terklehopper worked on rocket fuel at Vandenberg.

All of them made it a point to gather together and share ideas at least twice a year.

———

Most of Doctor Schock's Carnival was auctioned off after the authorities shut the place down. The rides, midway games, and displays are peppered amongst traveling fairs all over the western hemisphere.

Everyone working there was a missing person from a jurisdiction the carnival had visited in the past. It took some time, but they all made it back to their homes. Most had gaps in their memories and provided no details about their time with Doctor Schock.

Sheldon Phlipworth disappeared from the carnival grounds moments after Doctor Schock's demise. Months later he was seen boarding an ocean liner bound for Europe. It was rumored he found a grand position with the Cirque d'Hiver.

Pumm Pumm stayed at the Barrington Estate for a short time, then he was returned to the Congo via a program with the Nature's Trust. This program had been set into motion a year earlier through a series of letters between the principles of the trust and one Pummley Pummeroy, an associate of Doctor Schock. The final bits of the agreement were settled by Tank Barrington with some help from the anthropology department at Springton College.

The gorilla was overjoyed to head to the jungle.

———

James Remmington's dealerships continued to do well, and he quickly recovered his losses from bankrolling the live broadcast of the Springton 50. He stepped down from his position with the Springton Board of Supervisors and instead spent his extra time and money developing after school sports programs for the poorer neighborhoods in the county.

And after he graduated, Chad Remmington joined his father in the family business. During the sixties, when Remmington Ford was moving all the Mustangs they could stock, it was Chad who convinced his father to open a new lot called Remmington Imports. The Remmingtons sold even more Volkswagen Beetles than Mustangs.

Robert Worthington had performed a lot of financial hijinks while he was under Schock's control. He managed to wriggle his way out of the fraud charges, claiming coercion. Though he avoided incarceration, the board of the Springton Commerce Bank and Trust tossed him out.

He moved his family to the only city with a bank willing hire him, Babson Park in Central Florida. There, he spent the next thirty years as Regional Manager of the Southern Labor Credit Union.

He hated it. So did his wife. Biff Remington stayed close to his parents and ended up managing a plant making plastic storage containers for food.

———

One week after the events at Doctor Schock's Carnival, Tank Barrington handed in his own typed work at school. He used the coin-operated typewriters downstairs in the library. It was slow going. His fingers were more than twenty years old, but they were new to the user. Speech, however, came quickly.

Tank spent most of his time at the library, a most remarkable place. It seemed odd there weren't throngs of people inside. He recalled a higher headcount waiting in line for the *Freefall* than here amongst the books.

He used to get books from the doctor, but he didn't get to choose them. Now, he smiled each time he felt the rolling bearings of the card catalog drawers. Undeniable satisfaction when he found the volume he was after.

Moreover, he discovered related works he didn't even know existed on the same shelf. It was exhilarating.

His father, Nigel Barrington, managed to avoid a scandal after the carnival. He held onto his positions as mayor and chair of the Board of supervisors. But to recoup his losses from financing Doctor Schock's attempt to take over the world, Barrington pushed production hard at his factory.

Things used to be terrible at Barrington Birdies, makers of the world's most durable shuttlecocks. Now, they were worse.

Nigel Barrington's son, Tank, had been spending more time at the factory lately. Exploring the offices. Talking with the managers. This made Nigel Barrington think his boy was finally coming around to his way of thinking.

That hope fell apart one morning when Tank walked into his father's home office and told him calmly about all the information and hard evidence he'd gathered.

Shady finances.

Unsafe working conditions.

Poverty-level, under-the-table pay for the workers at the factory.

He pushed a stack of file folders containing a plan and timeline to clean it all up across his father's desk. If it wasn't implemented, he'd go to the authorities.

Nigel Barrington sat for a moment, fuming. Then he stood and walked around the desk to his son, where they stood face to face.

"My word," he said, "you are dumber than I

thought. Do you really think I'm going to do any of this? With *my* factory? *My* people?"

Tank's eyes locked onto his father's. He rose over him, huffing. He pounded his arms on his chest and threw them over his head, never breaking eye contact as he bared his teeth and broke into a high-pitched howl.

Nigel Barrington cowered. From that moment, he was no longer in charge.

At the factory, improvements come quickly.

———

Years later, the gorilla who had returned to the Congo had few memories of his life in Springton. He didn't recall his name, because gorillas never used them. He lived simply, enjoying each day.

And his favorite time was in the mornings when the mist was beginning to rise. He'd hear a rustle in the foliage. Noises made by creatures who, with all their hearts, believed they moved in silence.

The ape played along. Not moving, pretending not to notice as the sounds drew closer. Then, all three of his small gorilla children tackled him. He'd roll with them in the dirt and leaves under the watchful eyes of their mother.

And all of them were happy.

THE END

Trivia

Doctor Schock's Carnival Facts and Trivia

- *Doctor Schock's Carnival* is one of only two features with Harold J. Kerr serving as writer, producer, and director. The other was *Phantom Rider of the Pony Express* (1962).
- In 1971 (more than a decade after its release), this movie and two others from World Cinema Group were serialized in *Weird Adventure Magazine*. Those pages are reprinted here. The other two films were *Drag Strip Zombie Massacre* (1968) and *Bog Fiends* (1970).
- Most of the shots featuring carnival rides and midway games came from stock footage. The few carnival scenes featuring the cast were shot in one night at the Los Angeles County Fair. Kerr captured most of these scenes from a lot adjacent to the fairgrounds where the midway and rides were visible just past a fence.

- The Bendix Elecrojector was indeed available on the Dodge D-500, but it was not reliable. Only 35 were sold and most of them were retrofitted with 4-barrel carburetors. The patents for the Electrojector were sold to Bosch, who developed the system further. By the late sixties, *Bosch Fuel Injection* was featured in Mercedes-Benz, Porsche, and most other European cars.

- The sound effect for Schock's Brain Beam is the fog horn from Long Beach Harbor in California sped up to ten times normal speed.

- A large streak in the paint on the back wall is evidence that Schock's Research and Development rooms, the broadcast booth at the Speedway, the work shed where the Lab Rats develop the Max Drive, and the employee storage trailers were all redresses of the same set.

- Doctor Schock's Ultimate Brain Beam Helmet was a heavy gauge steel full-brim hard hat from the 1920s. They peppered it with vacuum tubes and holiday lights. It weighed nearly ten pounds and was painful, so actor Vincent Barbi refused to wear it during rehearsals and limited each scene with the helmet to a single take.

- If Pumm Pumm looks familiar, it's because suit performer George Barrows wore the same ape costume in *Gorilla at Large* (1954), *The Ghost in the Invisible Bikini* (1966), and many other films and television shows. In Phil Tucker's *Robot Monster* (1953), Barrows

used the same suit but topped it with a
space helmet rather than the gorilla head.

www.ingramcontent.com/pod-product-compliance
Lightning Source LLC
Chambersburg PA
CBHW010932120626
46552CB00009B/3222

* 9 7 8 1 9 6 6 0 3 7 5 8 3 *

Savage, colossal worms! Scientists call them *planaria giganticus*. You will call them MONSTERS! Smothering everything!
Devouring everyone! Science can't kill them! The army can't defeat them! Run or be crushed under the slimy attack of...GIGANTICUS!

Turn this book over for second complete novel

WORLD
CINEMA
GROUP

PRESENTS

Giganticus!

BRET NELSON

Encyclopocalypse Publications
www.encyclopocalypse.com

Foreword

I was an assistant in Dick Rubin's prop shop at the time, but he was in between pictures, so I joined the crew for this quicky monster movie at World Cinema Group - *Giganticus.*

If I remember right, this was Bill Sternbaum's first or second time as a director. (*It was his first.—Ed.*) But he was a great writer and he'd been on film sets most of his life, so he did just fine in the director's chair. Not green at all.

We didn't have much money or time, but that was typical. Everyone did their best with what they had. In most of the shots, the giant worms were flat pieces of latex around two feet wide. We had a little paint on

Giganticus! *Title card*
(1971)

them, so they'd catch the light better and not look like a surgical glove. They were covered in some kind of slime, might have been petroleum jelly or maybe methylcellulose. Anyway, we piled them up about ten high and attached some monofilament to the corners of the ones in the middle. Tugging on those moved

the whole stack around and if we piled them up just right, the top ones would slide down the heap right toward the camera.

We filmed that with a camera running at double speed, and they moved nice and slow and goopy. Dragged them through miniature sets, too. Like model railroaders use, and that all looked pretty good.

What didn't look good was the rear projection shots. Glad that wasn't my department. The production was really counting on that system for a lot of the picture, but their projection setup was lousy. It was the in-house rig at this little studio they rented and I'm pretty sure it was only made to run scenery behind the back windshield of a car.

The screen wasn't big enough to have more than four actors in front of it, and even then it was too hard to light the people on that small studio floor. This process is supposed to take two things, the plate and the actors, and shoot them through one lens so the two things turn into one scene.

Instead. our two things looked like two scenes stacked in front of each other. There's even a couple of shots where you can see the actor's shadow on the rear projection screen.

They did a few split screens and mattes to get our soldiers up against the worms, but they were counting on that rear projection for most of the shots and it didn't work. That's why there's so much cross cutting in the battle scenes.

Still, in the end, it was a low budget giant bug movie, so I don't think anybody really cared.

Oh, another thing that really worked was that huge flatworm in the big tank at the science lab. There was no water in that tank, but it looked like there was. It really did, even when you stood next to it. Justin did this remarkable trick with moving gels and lights

on wires, then reflecting them off a shallow pan of peroxide. It just looked great. (*He's talking about cinematographer Justin Ferraro.—Ed.*)

That meant we didn't have to worry about the giant worm prop getting wet or filling that massive tank. That beast was heavy though, big piece of rubber painted up to look like flesh. There were a couple of bladders in it and when we pushed and pulled on bicycle pumps, it moved just a little. Looked like a real, giant worm clinging to the side of the tank.

-Robert Terry (March, 2025)
Past Vice-Chair, Visual Effects Society
Los Angeles Section

WORLD
CINEMA
GROUP
PRESENTS

Giganticus!

In 1892, naturalist Herbert Lansen led an expedition down uncharted forks of the Amazon River in search of new species of wildlife, particularly insects. The journey was made possible by a generous grant from the American Natural History Museum.

Among his many discoveries on that trip was an area of approximately sixteen acres, almost completely surrounded by a long turn in the river. This "pocket," as Lansen called it, differed in wildlife, foliage, and other features from the rest of the jungle, even when compared to the area just on the opposite banks. With so many unique aspects, Lansen felt the area merited a separate expedition devoted to its exploration exclusively. He took careful notes as to its location and continued his trek.

Seven years later Lansen returned to the Amazon, but the rubber boom had taken its toll on the landscape. He was unable to find the particular forks that led him to the pocket. Over the following decades, no less than twelve expeditions, three led by Lansen himself, got nowhere closer to finding it. After his death in 1928, Lansen's Pocket became little more than a curiosity discussed by naturalists and cartographers. Some even argued Herbert Lansen made the whole thing up to guarantee funding for his future expeditions.

-Excerpt from:
Primer on Turn-of-the-Century Explorers
by Hermione Marchworth, EdD
Oxford University Press, 1957

A converted tool and die plant just outside the beltway in Washington, DC housed Kincaid Innovation. There were smaller offices and plants around the country, but this was the main facility, located a few miles away from the modest house where Drs. Michael and Evelyn Kincaid made their home.

If you included the initials for all their credentials (doctorates, certifications, and the like) after their names, each would fill two typed lines. They'd been part of, and in many cases responsible for, most of the advances in science and medicine over the last decade, starting with their first patent in 1960 for the Kincaid Micro-solenoid.

Every Tuesday they met with Eddie Beaumont in the facility's glass-walled conference room to go through their calendars and correspondence. Beaumont had been their right hand since the beginning. He could have had his own string of doctorates if he cared to, but he found the processes of discovery and invention more rewarding than any time he'd ever spent in academia.

This morning, he faced the near-impossible task of planning the Kincaids' schedules. Michael Kincaid

was more focused than usual. Evelyn scratched notes across a document.

"Those notes don't have anything to do with our datebook, do they?" asked Michael.

"Absolutely not," said Evelyn. "Well, kind of. If we want this report for Reese Electronics delivered on time, I've got to get this summary done today. That deadline is on the calendar. So, I'm working on a calendar thing. You buying that?"

"Absolutely not," said Michael.

Reese Electronics hired Kincaid Innovation to stress test their prototype heat-resistant condensers. Reese's government contract required third party confirmation of every claim. The reporting had to be precise.

"The photos and samples are packaged," said Eddie. "Ready for shipping to Reese. Once your summary is finished, the whole thing can go out in one box." He held up his copy of the calendar, hoping to draw attention away from the Reese report. "Moving to next month. Our new CT Scanner is coming into service at New York Medical College. I got a call from Janine Todd, you remember her, the one in charge."

"Of course," said Mike.

"They're having a press thing on the 15th about their new imaging center," said Eddie. "Doctor Todd is going to be there, and she'd like both of you to be there, too. They want everyone to pose in front of the gizmo."

"I signed off on the installation last week," said Evelyn. "They aren't going to wait another month to start using it, are they?"

"They called with a few maintenance questions yesterday," said Michael. "It's in daily operation, working well. The Public Relations people are packaging an event is all. We can be there for some pictures."

"There had better be food," said Evelyn. "And not hospital food."

"And the last calendar note," said Eddie, taking back the meeting, "You're invited to the United Nations to hear Monica Sherman's speech to the general assembly on clean nuclear energy. It's the day after the hospital thing, so if you stay over one night in New York it works out. Doctor Sherman wants to know if you can be there for moral support."

"She's got it," said Evelyn. "It's 1970, a brand-new decade for crying out loud. You'd think these so-called 'world leaders' would understand the potential for atomic energy by now." Michael nodded in agreement.

"Okay," said Eddie. "That leaves the mail. It's the usual stuff." He tapped the neat piles on the table in front of him. "Letters from school kids doing reports, equipment catalogs -"

"Is that one from Pratt and Whitney?" asked Evelyn, eyeing the stack.

"Yup."

"Gimme."

Eddie tossed it to her, and she paged through it. "Digital readouts," she whispered. "Yummy."

"The rest of these are invoices and such. I'll send them along to accounts," said Eddie. "One exception, though. There's this poor thing." He held up a bent, weathered envelope. "The return address is smeared, but it's gotta be from Sam Browning, right?"

Michael Kincaid took the letter and turned it over in his hands. "It's beat up and there's postage from all over. Ah, this big mark is from the station in Blumenau. Gotta be Sam."

"How does he get mail out of the middle of the Amazon jungle, anyway?" asked Eddie.

"He gives his correspondence to the people who run his supply boat," said Evelyn. "It's that outfit Sam

always uses, Harrington Charters. They get it to the U.S. Post Station in Blumenau, and from there it weaves its way here. Takes weeks."

"Wow," said Michael, reading the water-stained pages he'd extracted from the envelope. "Listen to this..."

> Dear Mike and Evelyn,
>
> This is the letter I've been hoping to write since I arrived in the Amazon last year. I'm standing in Lansen's Pocket. I've checked the location against every article and book about the 1892 expedition, even photostats of Herbert Lansen's original journal pages.
>
> The river makes a nearly straight run of 12 miles, with bank variations under two yards, then a forty degree turn to the southwest, just like it's supposed to. Finally, there's the long curve bordering 16 acres of jungle flats with the right mix of ponds, odd bugs, and strange plants. And the locals' oral history tells of a visit all those years ago.
>
> If I'm right (and that is an "if" because Lansen didn't carve his initials on a tree) you should get down here. I need help verifying everything. You're the only people I trust to keep this quiet.
>
> Lansen was right. There's enough new species and wonder in every square foot of this place to fill a set of encyclopedias. The last thing we need is a bunch of gloryhounds stomping through and dropping every critter they find in a kill jar.
>
> I've enclosed the series of steps you'll need to go through to respond to this letter. I await your reply.
>
> Yours,
> Sam Browning

"If anyone's going to find Lansen's Pocket, it's Sam Browning," said Evelyn. "He's spent most of his life in a tent someplace."

"The Smithsonian is bankrolling his Amazon ex-

cursion," said Michael. "If he's right, they're going to get more than their money's worth."

"And he won't lose the location like Lansen did," said Eddie. "Sam will have already made hyper-accurate maps on how to get there. And with you two backing him up on the initial findings, the Smithsonian will bend over backwards to protect the site."

———

In the weeks that followed, the report for Reese Electronics was delivered on time, the New York Medical College press party featured excellent catering, and Doctor Monica Sherman got the right people talking at the UN.

And by the time these events were finished, Eddie Beaumont had completed arrangements for himself and the Kincaids to go on a thirty-day excursion into the Amazon.

The trip began with a seven-hour Braniff flight from Dulles to Lima Airport, arriving in the early evening. They were only in town long enough to eat and collapse into bed at a hotel. Travel started again at dawn.

Fog or clouds might have ended their journey, as the pilots needed absolute visual clarity to fly over the peaks and trees of the Andes. Fortunately, the morning brought clear skies, so under the rising sun they piled their gear and themselves into a Faucett Airlines DC-6 and took off at 7:03am.

They had to fly at 20,000 feet to get over the mountains. The last time they made this trip was eight years ago in a bent up old Douglas DC-4. The crew passed around oxygen with the peanuts to make sure no one passed out in the unpressurized cabin.

Things went much smoother this time.

Flying east out of Lima, there were only two colors

visible through the plane windows: the blue sky above and the brown landscape below. As the altitude increased and the mountains got closer, the snowy peaks of the Andes added a white stripe to the tableau.

The whites and browns vanished completely once the plane flew past the peaks. They were replaced by the green of the jungle. A seamless emerald floor stretching all the way to the horizon.

They had to land in Pucallpa for refueling. Ribbons of blue appeared in the endless jade once the plane started its descent. Streams that started high above in the snow wove together to become the Amazon and its countless forks and tributaries. Somewhere in the endless tangle of water and vines, Sam Browning was mapping Lansen's Pocket.

It took close to an hour for the fuel to be hand-pumped from steel drums. Then another takeoff and another hour of flight time got them to their true destination, the Iquitos Airport.

For the team from Kincaid Innovation, it would be small boats from here on. Tremendous ferries and aircraft left Iquitos every few hours, but these were all headed west. To the brown landscape of civilization.

Eddie Beaumont and the Kincaids were journeying east, deeper into the green. The next morning, a chartered launch was due to take them on the next leg of their journey.

That left the evening free. They had a good meal, chicken and vegetables in a rich broth with corn cakes called *arepas*. They also had a good sleep. The hotel had excellent beds, and everyone was exhausted from their travels.

And early the next morning, seated in the hotel café, they found Sam Browning sipping coffee. "Let's have breakfast. I haven't had a fresh egg in ages," he said. "But we've got to get moving right after."

2

Browning had decided to bring them to Lansen's Pocket himself. His boat was big enough for all four of them to be comfortable.

Everyone but Browning sat in padded swivel seats. He sat up front steering the boat. They towed small barge for all the gear. "Don't be shy about stretching out," said Browning. "Like I said, Lansen's Pocket is three days out."

Mike did math. "We marked out thirty days for this. There's two days on each side for the flights between the States and South America, then three days each side on the river, that means we've got twenty days to work the site."

"Gold star, Dr. Kincaid," said Evelyn.

Eddie pulled his coat collar up. "Rain's coming," he said.

"All the time," said Browning. "Get used to being wet. Don't take equipment out of the tents and don't bring wet coats or shoes into the tents."

"Not to be insulting, Sam, but there's an odor about you," said Mike. "And I'm not talking about camping smells."

"Yeah," said Evelyn. "Kind of like candles. What is that?"

Browning pulled a jar of grey paste from a bag at his feet and tossed it to Mike. "This is a salve made from boiling down the leaves of an Araza Tree."

"Odd ingredient for jam," said Eddie.

"Pass that around and you won't find it odd at all," said Browning. "In fact, you'll adore smelling this way. Put a little smear of the stuff where you perspire. Under your arms, your sternum, anyplace you sweat. And presto, no bugs. They won't come near you."

"I'm for that!" said Eddie. "These mosquitos are eating me alive. One of them stole my wallet."

"You must have made contact with the locals to pick up a trick like this," said Mike, smearing the paste on his neck.

"I have. There's a good-sized village a little ways down river from the pocket. They're the closest neighbors. I can't say for certain if they are Wajapi people, but they share a similar language."

———

Three days on the river. Three days of odd greenery moving past the boat and rain falling down. Creatures among the vines chattered joyfully as they ate or shrieked horribly as they were eaten.

The canopy of intersecting treetops above meant constant shade and remarkable humidity. Occasionally the rain stopped, and the canopy revealed a gap that let in a shaft of the brightest sunlight ever known. Eddie called it "A cylinder of pure radiance, like something out of legend marking the resting place of a God."

Everyone else called it light.

Browning had created hyper-detailed maps of the forks in the river leading to Lansen's Pocket. For each turning there were careful drawings of the permanent features. These were the only way to stay on course.

There weren't enough stones to pile on the banks of the correct turns. The trees along the river may have seemed an obvious solution, but carving signs into them would kill them. The birds stole anything tied around the trunks or hung from the branches. Rain washed away paint or stakes.

So, any time the river offered turning options, Browning studied the maps in his leather-bound portfolio and knew the way to go. He'd even noted the best places to set camp for the two nights along the way.

And on the third day, they traveled a nearly straight run of 12 miles, then made a forty degree turn to the southwest. Finally, there was the long curve bordering 16 acres of jungle flats.

Browning turned the boat toward a low section of the bank and said, "Welcome to Lansen's Pocket."

———

A dozen large tents stood in a clearing twenty yards from the riverbank. Lighting and equipment got power from five generators. This could hardly be called "roughing it."

Two tents outfitted for living quarters were given to the Kincaids and Eddie Beaumont. Following their days-long river trip, everyone slept hard on their cots.

The next morning, after a breakfast of powdered eggs, fresh mango, and instant coffee, Browning led a tour. The plants and trees were lush here, so even though the pocket covered sixteen acres, only a few yards were visible at a time. The area housing the

camp and lengthy runs along the riverbank were the only clear places.

"The river narrows here, but the current gets slower," said Browning, walking Evelyn, Mike, and Eddie around the bank. "That's not the way rivers work, so it was one of the first mysteries I set out to solve."

"Bet that's what all the scuba gear back at camp is for," said Eddie.

"It is," said Browning. He pointed to a yellow Meranti Tree on the opposite bank, the only one of its kind for miles. An excellent landmark. "Straight out from here, right in the center, there's a drop off. But before you hit bottom, there's an outcropping of rock. A shelf, runs for about a mile. There's a cave under it. A flooded, underwater cave. Huge. Couldn't find the end or the edges."

"That's why the current is slow," said Evelyn. "The river feeds the equivalent volume of a lake, but it's underground. Amazing."

"Sure amazed me," said Browning. "Cave diving is a specialized, dangerous thing. So, I asked around and found the Casimiro brothers from São Paulo, Leandro and Rodrigo. They're on a gear run now, but you'll meet them tonight. They are two of fifteen people on the planet who understand the challenges of cave diving. It's nothing like the ocean. The ocean doesn't have a ceiling"

"Or tunnels or pinch points," said Eddie. "No, thank you. I'll stay up top and catalog everything, if that's all right."

"Sounds great," said Browning.

Evelyn and Mike knelt by the water's edge. "You're right about the current," said Mike, his hand sweeping the surface. "It's nearly still."

"And so clear," said Evelyn. "Is this water as pure as it looks?"

"Clean clean," said Browning. "Better than you'd get from *Source Perrier*."

"Evelyn and I are both certified for scuba, but we've never done a cave," said Mike. "Not sure how useful we can be."

"Those Sãu Paulo boys are great at what they do," said Browning. "They've got the mapping and specimen collection covered. I need your help on the analytical side so we can classify those specimens. Plus, there's acres to explore up here."

Eddie wandered toward the jungle's edge. He found a pond no wider than a kiddie pool. "Hey Sam," he called. "Are there a lot of these little ponds?"

"Pretty, aren't they? They're a feature Lansen noted in his journals. I've found eight of them so far, each a different size and shape."

Evelyn joined Eddie at the pond. "How deep are they?"

"Don't fall in. Goes all the way down. These are shafts that drop into the underwater cave system. From below, you'll see columns of light coming in from these ponds. You should go on a dive with the Casimiros and have a look."

"This place is entirely remarkable," said Mike. He joined the others and peered into the pond. "What else have you found down there, Sam?"

"Wonders," said Browning. "Just like up here."

Each day the group found previously unseen specimens of plants, fungi, insects, fish, and mollusks. All needed study and identification. For some, that would happen in the camp's research tent. Others were packed carefully to be carried back to the Kincaid's lab in Washington, DC.

It was hard work in tough conditions. The wet and the heat never let up.

By the eleventh day, Eddie Beaumont felt off-kilter. Evelyn and Sam had gone on a dive with the Casimiros, leaving Mike and Eddie to get caught up indexing the microscope slides.

In the large research tent, they worked in silence. Eddie took frequent pauses to tilt back his head, peel off his glasses, and squeeze the bridge of his nose.

"You feeling all right?" asked Mike.

"Homesick, probably," said Eddie. "All the rainy days hunched over these slides. The hissing bugs and the screaming animals. It's getting to me. I'll be okay, though. We're more than half done."

"At least we've got enough work to fill the time."

"You're right there." Eddie pointed out the crates stacked behind him. "And all the samples we've packed up will keep us busy for months back home." Eddie leaned in his chair and smiled. "Ah, *home*. You know what I miss most?"

Mike didn't look up from his microscope. "This morning you said it was toast and jam."

"No, I'm over that. It's the radio. There's this college station out of Philly. They play music you don't hear anywhere else. I can get it through the big antenna on the roof back in DC. I miss that music more than my real bed."

"Well, it won't be long before you have your radio again," said Mike, tucking his completed slide to a numbered slot in the container. "And the record store next that hamburger place you like."

"For crying out loud, Mike. Did you have to bring up burgers?"

Two days later, Eddie's head hung even lower. In the research tent, Evelyn checked his eyes and throat after a coughing fit.

"Look at you," she said. "You're dehydrated. More water, lots of it."

"I boiled a pot. Should be cool enough to drink in a bit."

"Boiled? You still don't trust the water?" asked Evelyn. "I've had it every day since we got here. So has Mike. No problems."

"Remember a few years back when I went to Borneo?" said Eddie, dabbing his nose with a bit of cloth. "I got dysentery. I was a human sluice for a week. Promised myself I'd never have river water again; not without some kind of purification."

"It's different here," said Evelyn, feeling his forehead. "The locals are downstream and it's clear for twenty miles upstream. And besides, you're the only one who has this cold, or whatever it is. We'd all have it if the water carried microscopic nasties."

Mike entered the tent carrying boxes filled with catch nets. Each had a tangle of butterflies and beetles. "Hello all. This is the last bunch from the east quadrant. We've seen a lot of these bugs already, but there's about thirty new ones." He put them down and got a good look at Eddie. "You still feeling lousy?"

"No fever, but our boy has a sniffle and a cough," said Evelyn.

"Between the humidity, the travel, and whatever molds are here, it's no wonder I'm sick." Eddie went back to filling out index cards. "Sam went down river to visit the locals this morning. I asked him to check if they had any home remedies."

He didn't see Sam Browning enter the tent.

"Some kind of tea maybe," said Eddie.

"They have no medicinal teas," said Browning.

"Cripes, Sam," said Eddie. "How long have you been there?"

"Moments. Hello all, full house in the research tent, eh?"

"If there's no tea, maybe we can try leeches," said Mike.

"Or blistering," said Evelyn.

Browning sat down. "I've had them both. Leeches in Gambia and blistering in Dubai. I can't recommend either one. But I did learn something from the neighbors. Quite a lot, actually."

The Kincaids found chairs. Eddie turned away from his work and toward Browning.

"This morning," said Browning, "I asked around about sinus remedies. It led to a long talk with several of the local people down river. And that talk led to an even longer sit-down with the elders, then lots of chats with others all over the village."

"Boy, this local remedy must be a complicated recipe," said Mike.

"Not complicated at all," said Browning. "Because they don't have any local remedies. I asked what they did for a stuffy nose or a fever, and they didn't understand what I was talking about."

"I don't understand what you're talking about, either," said Eddie.

"Like any culture, the people in the village have roles in the community," said Browning. "Builders, hunters, artists. But nobody makes medicine."

"What happens if someone gets sick?" asked Evelyn.

"Everyone makes things like bug repellent and soaps for themselves. And they have healers who set broken bones and bind up lacerations. But no one treats illness. Because there *is no illness*. I've checked with thirty people so far and none of them have ever been sick. Or known anyone who has been sick."

"That can't be right," said Mike.

"I'm telling you; they have no words for *ill* or *dis-*

ease. They understand *injury* but not *infection*. When I described Eddie's symptoms, they thought he was simply a weakling."

"Hey!" said Eddie.

And for the next three days, their research shifted focus to the local people down the river.

———

In the laboratory tent, Evelyn Kincaid tore a paper strip from the analyzer and scrutinized the final numbers. For a minute, the only sound was the bap-bap-bap of the generator outside.

She shut down the equipment then took the strip and a thick file folder to the mess tent where the Eddie, Sam, and her husband were having their lunch.

On her arrival, Mike said "There's a plate there for you. And juice if you want some."

"Please," said Evelyn. She sat, organized her papers and had a few mango chunks.

Mike brought her a cup of maracuja juice. "How are the numbers coming? You need any help?" he asked.

"Done. Have a look," she said between bites. "These are the final results and there's no doubt. It's the water. It's why no one here gets sick."

Browning and Eddie gathered around as Mike spread the file's contents on the table. Evelyn continued. "There's an enzyme that props up your endocrine system. Illness doesn't stand a chance. Your lymphatic vessels, spleen, all of it works at least a third more efficiently than what we call 'nominal.' The water is tuned for health, and they've been drinking it and soaking in it since birth."

"Even longer," said Eddie, "The mothers drink the water. The exposure is prenatal."

"What about longevity?" asked Browning.

15

"They aren't immortal, but they live longer," said Evelyn. She pointed out the appropriate graph. "Aging works the same as anywhere else. That said, they aren't passing due to disease or infection. Think of how many people die of pneumonia - they don't here."

Mike paced the room. "So why? What has this water got that other water doesn't?" He got ready for a long think, but Evelyn cut it short.

"Coral," she said, finishing her sandwich.

"Don't think I heard you right," said Eddie. "Coral? This is fresh water, sourced from the Andes, not the sea."

"You are correct. But so is she," said Browning. "Do you remember those structures we brought up from the underwater caves about a week ago? The ones we thought looked like coral?"

"Yes," said Eddie. "Have you finished the testing?"

"I have," said Browning. "They look like coral because they are coral. Freshwater coral."

"There's tons of it," said Mike. "Vast beds cover most of the cave floor, I saw them myself. Must be thousands of years old."

"I've been running tests on the samples ever since Sam identified them," said Evelyn. "Results are conclusive. The corals filter this water and add a string of proteins I won't pretend to understand... yet. But it's what gives the water this unique enzyme profile."

"So, what do you think, Mike?" asked Eddie.

"I think we need to spend the rest of our time here learning all we can about these corals," said Mike. "Then we need to package that information along with living samples and head to Washington."

"I agree," said Browning. "But we have to be guarded in our studies and sampling. This is the only

place on Earth with these conditions. We can't turn it into the only place that *used to* have these conditions."

"Yes," said Evelyn. "Every piece we remove should be budding and healthy, and its removal should in no way threaten the larger bed."

"All right let's put together a plan and a schedule," said Mike.

Eddie chugged down the first glass of river water he'd had in years. "Wow," he said. "We may have found a cure for everything."

3

Dr. Monica Sherman's home base was a facility she led in northwestern Arkansas called SEFOR. Most people misconstrued the name as "C-4," the alphanumerical designation for a recently-developed explosive. It was, instead, an acronym for *Southwest Experimental Fast Oxide Reactor.*

The facility's name didn't matter to Dr. Sherman. "Paper-pusher gobbledygook," she called it. The people in the government accounting offices who named things loved using initials and numbers to make it sound like they were part of a Captain Video future instead of their actual desk-jockey posts.

Besides, most of what the government knew about SEFOR was a lie.

Cover story: Dr. Sherman and her team came to this short-term project facility to test cooling methods for nuclear cores. Both day-to-day operations and emergency situations needed fast cooling technology. A few years back, her group created the oxide fuel and liquid sodium configurations that became the world standard for fast cooling. Now they were making them better.

Reality: This facility wasn't working on cooling

systems. It was working on free, clean energy to save the world. Less than 70 miles away heavy equipment ran day and night at the future site of Arkansas Nuclear One (AN1). Electricity for millions of people. And when they power it up four years from now, the energy output will be 60% higher than anyone expected.

All thanks to the quiet work Monica Sherman and her team were doing at SEFOR.

As the construction teams dug the foundation for AN1, a series of underground labs were created to test the plant's equipment, and part of those tests meant working with SEFOR. Some of those tests were off the books, creating the future.

To make a better future for everyone on Earth, they had to keep things quiet. Any number of small-minded bureaucrats or generals might ruin everything if they got close. Atomic power was a leap in human progress unseen since people began forging metals. And Dr. Sherman could see the entire path forward as clearly as she saw the sunrise. Everything from transportation to breakfast cereal was about to become better.

If she and her team were left alone.

She led a small group of key researchers and scientists, just eight people. Most of them had been working together for more than a decade. A few, like her lab techs Steve Smith and Barry Johnson, had been with her even longer.

They had discovered a better way to enrich uranium, and the fewer people involved in these nascent stages the better. It was vital to keep bad operators, even our own government and military, in the dark until Dr. Sherman's triple-enriched uranium had a repeatable, stable process to create and contain it.

In four years, this uranium will fuel AN1. The beginning of free energy for all. Smaller, shoebox ver-

sions of the plant with a core the size of a nickel could provide power to a small village anywhere on the planet. With that, the concept of scarcity, of a third world, vanished.

As long as Dr. Sherman and her team were left alone.

Triple-enriched uranium lasted forever. The containment system had no moving parts, so it never wore out. But efficient things that last forever are unpopular with the governments and businesses who pay for their development. They count on things wearing out, so people buy more. That's commerce. That's jobs.

That's nonsense, thought Monica Sherman. *Spend the time and money on other things, because now we can keep the lights on for free.*

But she needed another year to perfect the process. To make the uranium and the containment system usable *only* for energy, and impossible to use for war. Until then, they had to keep a lid on what they were really doing at SEFOR.

How? By making everything they did seem as complicated and dull as possible.

———

Out of 102 samples of living freshwater coral, 93 survived the trip home.

The Kincaids reached out to a pair of high-ranking contacts in the United States Government - Felicia Ward at the Department of Health, Education, and Welfare and Albert Sawyer at the Department of the Interior. Old friends who immediately grasped the potential of freshwater coral. Ward agreed to underwrite a research facility. Sawyer found a place to build it.

Lake Dardanelle State Park in Pope County, Ar-

kansas became the home of the United States Science Dome. There, the Kincaids were in charge, assisted by a small army of research scientists and lab technicians.

Spherical structures sprung up like giant mushrooms on the eastern shore of Lake Dardanelle. The Army Corps of Engineers had been working with Geodesics, Inc. to build armed forces housing and Geodesics wanted to create something on a much larger scale, so Albert Sawyer brought them in on the Science Dome project. They did the job at cost because it gave them the opportunity to prove they could build an entire complex.

The main building was large enough to be an airplane hangar. Instead, it held sixteen different labs. Three of the smaller domes held aquariums, some piped together and others operating independently.

Though it was called a "lake," Dardanelle was actually part of the Arkansas River. The slow currents emulated the conditions in the Amazon. A sizable, clear-sided dome extended over the shoreline, so a section of the riverbank was indoors. This section and another of similar size outside were the only coral beds in naturally occurring environments. The rest of the corals were in the controlled aquarium tanks.

The corals thrived, but there was no way of knowing if they'd create healing waters in their new home.

———

When Kincaid Innovation partners with the government, it doesn't take long for the reporters to get wind of it. So, a press conference was called.

Mike's face was hidden because there were so many microphones on the dais. They had to put the news cameras on risers to see him.

Behind him, next to wall of images and charts, stood Eddie Beaumont. He held the grave responsibility of using a pointer to direct the press to the appropriate visual aide.

Doctor Evelyn Kincaid took notes as the questions flew at them and tracked the corrections she'd have to distribute because Mike's off-the-cuff answers were often seasoned with too much optimism.

Albert Sawyer and Felicia Ward were there to answer questions related to the Government first hand. One of the first questions was directed at Ward, as all of the reporters wanted to know why the project was paid for with tax dollars.

"The money comes from an already-established fund for this kind of research. It's not new spending, it was set aside years ago. The potential outcome here is too great for a private entity to own and control," she said. "This way, the results will benefit all."

Marion Goldin from *CBS News* raised her hand. "Isn't that communism?" she asked. The other reporters laughed.

"No," said Sawyer. "Communists would put the corals to work in a factory."

Another reporter raised a pen. "Walter Sullivan, New York Times."

"Yes, Walter," said Evelyn. "Everyone's being so formal."

"Sorry, just minding my manners," said Sullivan. "From what we've heard, you found a cure for the common cold in the Amazon. True?"

"Not quite," said Mike. "And your readers at the *Times* are going to have to wait a year or two before we can say exactly what we've got."

That got a groan all around.

"I know, I know," said Mike. "Here's what I *can* say. We've found a naturally occurring process and if

we can learn enough about it, we may help people live a healthier life."

Voices and raised hands popped up all over the room. Evelyn pointed to a man in the back. "You've been waiting, go ahead."

"Michael Sneed, Chicago Tribune," said the man. "This sounds like an old ad for snake oil. Is there anything solid? Results you can give us today?"

"All we have now is potential," said Mike. "But if it goes the way I think it will, the benefits for mankind will be immeasurable."

"Immeasurable benefits?" said Eddie. "Geez, Mike, you are selling hard,"

"And there's no need for all that selling," said Sawyer. "We already bought it."

"All right," said Mike. "Here's what I *can* say. We went to the Amazon and found promising things there. We brought a few of them home with us and now we've got these promising things in our new lab. We are working now on unlocking their promises."

"Slowly and carefully," added Eddie. "You're doing well Mike, no exaggerations in those last few statements."

"Thanks. Well, that's it everyone. Make sure you grab a one-sheet, it's got the particulars. And hopefully, before the end of the year, we'll host another press conference and tell you how we've changed everything for the better."

The article Walter Sullivan wrote for the *New York Times* got picked up all over the world:

DATELINE: ARKANSAS - *Freshwater corals hailed as the discovery of the century! Specimens from the Amazon arrive at the newly christened United States Science Dome. Incredible healing properties could add decades to human life span...*

4

Soon, the aquarium tanks at the Science Dome showed traces of the mysterious proteins from the corals. The Kincaids got water analysis reports twice a day and reviewed them in their main lab.

"These numbers are rising," said Mike.

"Yes," said Evelyn. "Hope it means something good. There's so much we don't know."

"Time, my love. It takes time. Is Eddie back from DC yet?"

"His plane landed a while ago," said Evelyn. "He might be on campus by now."

Eddie Beaumont was splitting his time. Corals were the exclusive project at the Science Dome, but hundreds of other specimens from the Amazon were being studied at Kincaid Innovation back in Washington, DC. Eddie was in charge of wrangling researchers and their results at both locations.

"We're going to need more help," said Evelyn. "The rate of change around these corals is only going to increase. And these studies come twice a day already."

"Not sure I follow," said Mike. He stood with his empty cup and reached for hers. "Coffee?"

She squeezed his hand and shut her eyes tight. "Please." She fanned out one of the reports so she could see every page. "There are more things to classify every day. The changes in biology are filling so many pages. It's really stacking up."

Mike returned from the drink cart with a cup in each hand. "Aren't you a biologist?" he asked.

"You're funny. Thanks for the coffee because now I have a weapon."

He gave her a kiss. "I get what you're saying. It's the same for me. I've been spending so much time researching how to do this research that it gets in the way of the research. You're saying we need another biology lead."

"More specific, please."

Mike thought for a moment. "A microbiologist?"

"Closer," said Evelyn. "This is marine microbiology and ecology as well."

"Is pollution is a factor?"

"It's easy to conflate ecology and pollution," said Evelyn. "But ecology is about relationships."

"I see. This is about how organisms get along with each other. And their relationship with their environment."

The main door swung open, and Eddie Beaumont swept in with a banker's box in his hands. "Behold! I have returned."

"Eddie!" said Mike. "How are things back in DC?"

"Moving along on schedule," said Eddie. "Good group you've got over there. The beetles are already done, and the arachnids will be completed by the end of the week." He raised the box chin-high. "More importantly, where can I put this? And is there coffee? Answer the second question first."

"Coffee is on the cart by the window, and you can put the box anywhere," said Evelyn. "Is that the mail?"

"Yup." He plopped the box in front of her and went straight for the coffee. "I've already sent the bills and invoices to accounts. There's nothing time-sensitive in there. Look at your leisure."

"You didn't happen to see any resumes for microbiologists, did you?" asked Mike.

Eddie sipped his coffee then looked at the cup. "Whoever is making this needs to use two more scoops. And I didn't see any resumes from anyone. Are we hiring?"

"Yes," said Mike. "We need a microbiologist who specializes in marine life. They also need a deep understanding of ecology. That is, ecology defined as the interdependencies of tiny creatures and their environment." He looked to Evelyn for approval.

"Gold star, Doctor Kincaid," she said. "That's exactly who we need."

"Okay," said Eddie. "I'll call Gertie and see if she's busy."

There was a pause.

"Gertie?" said Mike.

"Doctor Gertrude Peterson," said Eddie. "Met her years ago on that trip to Fiji when we were field testing submersibles. Good friend, and she's always asking what you guys are up to."

Eddie pawed through his box of mail and tossed the latest issue of *National Geographic* onto the table. The cover image had Jacques Cousteau sunning on the deck of the Calypso. To his right, laughing at one of his jokes, was Gertrude Peterson.

"She's been with the Cousteau team lately," said Eddie.

"We know who she is," said Mike.

"Everyone knows who she is," said Evelyn. "You think you can track her down?"

"She called me a few days ago. Her Cousteau work is paused for now and she's back home. I'll

reach out. See you at dinner." With a small bow, Eddie left the room.

"Gertrude Peterson on our team... she'd be perfect," said Mike.

Evelyn smiled and paged through National Geographic. "And it's more proof of my theory."

"Which theory?"

"Monica Sherman, Janine Todd, Felicia Ward, and now Gertrude Peterson," said Evelyn. "All the brainy girls love Eddie Beaumont."

"That may be true, but he missed the best one," said Mike, taking her hands. "I got to this brainy girl first."

———

Each Monday at SEFOR Doctor Monica Sherman and her core team met behind closed doors for a briefing and bagels. "Our prototype cooling tower is fully integrated with the other equipment being tested at Arkansas Nuclear One," she said. "They want to start using small quantities of uranium to make certain everything works at scale."

"How small is small?" asked Barry Johnson.

"The schematics call for a single 10-inch cylinder," said Sherman. "But they want standing inventory, so they'll need several stored there. They also want me on site when they run the plant. More eyes on the process."

"Tell them the good part," said Steve Smith.

She held up a document. "We've been tasked by the Atomic Energy Commission to be the weigh station for the test cores. SEFOR has bonded assessment facilities, so the cores will come here first to get checked out, then transported to AN1 for inclusion in their stock."

Happy murmurs and smiles moved through all eight of the trusted team members. "Good, you get it," said Sherman. "We can include some triple-enriched cores in the deliveries. And as long as I'm there for the tests we've got everything covered. Barry, is your friend at AN1 still in charge of schedules and inventory?"

"Her name is Aveline Berger, and yes she's still in charge. She'll copy down whatever we give her, no questions asked. But maybe we should let her know what's up."

"Why?" asked Smith. "The fewer people in the know, the better. Our containment units are working great. As far as what's inside, it's either going to be a regular cylinder or a triple-enriched cylinder. We'll know by the number designation."

"I guess," said Johnson.

"The triple-enriched cores are safer, anyway," said Sherman. "Steve and Barry have been making runs out there in our cargo van for months now. The only change here is the cargo. Used to be parts for the cooling tower, now it's cores for the plant testing. This is all good news. The future is getting closer every day."

———

It only took three phone calls and one long dinner to get Doctor Gertrude Peterson to join the team at the Science Dome. And she was precisely what they needed.

Gertrude Peterson wasn't a button-down scientist like the Kincaids were used to working with. She always had bright tops and jeans or a peasant skirt under her lab coat. She had fresh ideas and a quick stride.

29

At the end of her first week, she stepped through the twenty-page report of her initial findings with the Kincaids and Eddie Beaumont in the conference area of the main dome.

"Like their salt-water relatives, these corals are filter feeders," she said. "The water moves, they take in what they need and trade proteins and other bits for it. If this river water and the water from the Amazon are enough alike, you'll get a like response from the coral."

"Understood," said Mike.

Peterson passed around a chart. "These are new numbers; new tests I'd like to run every week. There is a whole world in every drop of water. If you look close enough, keep zooming in, you'll see a micro-scopic realm of species and environments. This page shows a micro-scale comparison of this water to your samples from Lansen's Pocket."

It only took Evelyn a moment to see the value in this comparison. "This is great. There are similarities, but so many differences. I guess we weren't looking closely enough."

"What's it mean for the specimens?" asked Eddie.

"The coral is getting nutrients from an all-new diet," said Peterson. "They will certainly be healthy, but we can't be sure what they will give back to the water."

"We'll have to wait and see I suppose," said Mike.

———

"It's a little sniffle. This Arkansas weather plays hell with my allergies." Steve Smith dabbed his nose with his handkerchief then bumped the lever for the wipers again. The air was barely damp enough to mist the cargo van's windshield every couple of minutes while he drove.

The irregular sweep of the wipers, plus Smith's stuffy nose and cough, made Barry Johnson feel agitated in the passenger seat. "The Atomic Energy Commission said any health changes, especially respiratory changes, should get checked out," he said. "Damn, these runs make me nervous."

This was the fifth time Smith and Johnson delivered uranium to AN1. Smith always drove the cargo van, as Johnson had trouble working a clutch. He also had trouble feeling safe while hauling experimental radioactive material.

"What's there to be nervous about?" said Smith. "Everything is sealed. Isolated in back."

"I get that," said Johnson. "But it's an experimental container. It's triple-enriched uranium. Triple! And how old is this van? How do we *know* the containment is safe?"

"Stop it," said Smith. "Everything is insulated eight different ways. You've got a Geiger counter right there on the seat. Run it. Then maybe you'll calm down."

Johnson switched on the device and waved its probe. "Less than 40 CPM," he said. "Barely higher than background. We're good."

"See? Told you." Smith started a coughing spell. "Criminy. Can you pour me a sip of coffee? Might calm this cough." He covered his mouth with one hand, keeping the other tight on the top of the steering wheel.

"Coming up." Johnson pulled the plastic cup from the top of the thermos and set it between his knees. "Don't know why I'm such a worrywart. Should have taken that reading a while ago. Of course we're safe."

He unscrewed the top of the flask. It hissed and sprayed yellow fog into his face.

You're part right, thought Smith. *There's no danger from the radiation. But you aren't safe.* He lowered his

hand, revealing a micro-respirator clenched in his teeth. Johnson went limp and the thermos fell to the floorboards. It didn't spill because it never held any coffee. Only a lethal dose of halothane.

Smith rolled down the window and waited fifteen minutes for the air to clear.

In three days, he'd be in Cuba. By April, he'd return home to Kazan in the Motherland. There, he'd start using his real name again. He was looking forward to that. He hadn't been Feliks Pushkin for eighteen years.

But for a little while longer, he'd remain Steve Smith. He radioed ahead to Arkansas Nuclear One and adjusted their arrival time. The roads were wet. They were being careful, so the normal two-hour trip would be more like two-and-a-half.

He needed the extra time.

At the mile marker 1181, he turned the cargo van off the interstate and onto a tight service road. One mile along, well out of sight from any other vehicles, he arrived at a small, sheet metal building. It was marked as equipment storage for the power company.

It wasn't equipment storage for the power company. And no one ever used this road. And Smith had a key to the padlock holding the clamshell doors closed.

Inside the building, a three-wheeled all-terrain vehicle (ATV) with a small trailer waited. Inside the trailer was a hazmat suit, a hazardous materials carrier unit (about the size of a toaster oven), and a pair of grabbers along with other tools. Apart from those, the structure was empty.

He backed the van up to the building and got to work. First, he sealed himself in the hazmat suit. Next, he used the grabbers and a great deal of deter-

mination to transfer a ten-inch rod of triple-enriched uranium from the containment barrel in the back of the van to his smaller carrier unit.

The cylinder weighed 85 pounds, but he managed it. The Geiger counter confirmed the material was safely sealed away.

Next, he rolled the ATV and trailer out of the building then parked the van in their place. He left the hazmat suit, the tools, and his dead companion in the sealed payload of the van. He left the van in the sheet metal building, closed the clamshell doors, and locked it up.

Finally, he moved two discarded pallets leaning against the east side of the structure to the west side of the structure. A sign for the disposal team to clean up the building's contents.

Smith felt a lot more like his old Pushkin self as he strapped the containment unit down in the small trailer and covered it with a folded tarp. He drove the ATV down the service road away from the interstate. After half a mile the pavement stopped, and a gravel path carried him the rest of the way to the Arkansas River's bank.

There, tied off right where it was supposed to be, he found an aluminum launch with fishing gear. The empty cooler under the seat was designed to receive the hazardous materials carrier unit.

He ditched the ATV and trailer behind some brambles off the road then paddled the boat away from shore. His orders were to pose as a fisherman and work his way down the river. In time, he'd reach the main dock on the south side of Lake Dardanelle. A Winnebago with his comrades waited for him there. Over the next few days, they'd move through a series of cars and identities all the way to Florida.

Then to Cuba. A victory for the party.

A single pull on the cord started the outboard motor. *Got it on the first try*, he thought. *A good sign.*

He headed east along the river, secure in the knowledge that Steve Smith and Barry Johnson weren't even expected at their destination for another hour.

5

In the conference area of the main dome, the morning brief was wrapping up.

"You know, you've added a lot more than coral to the river," said Peterson.

"How's that?" asked Eddie.

"Stowaways. Microbial hitchhikers." Peterson opened a binder and pushed it to the center of the table for everyone to see. "Sorry, I've only got one of these. As you know, a coral bed is an ecosystem unto itself. There are thousands of creatures in it, smaller than you can see. And you gave this bunch a free trip to the States."

Peterson flipped through the tabbed sections of the binder. "Zooxanthellae, endozoicomonas, flat-worms, plankton. There's lots more. They've never tasted these waters before. Never been near the micro-bial life forms that have become their new neighbors. Everything will react to everything else, and those re-actions will shape how your coral behaves."

"I hope everyone gets along," said Mike.

"All we can do is extract every bit of data we can," said Evelyn. "Eventually a pattern will emerge."

"True," said Peterson. "And I promise... the pattern will surprise you."

———

As per the plan, Feliks Pushkin kept to the southern banks of Lake Dardanelle. This course kept his craft away from the construction crews and dredgers on the north shore, the future site of Arkansas Nuclear One.

A toy, he thought.

He had seen the plans for the grand nuclear towers under construction at Novovoronezh in central Russia. The sheer scope of that design put this paltry American facility to shame.

There were intermittent splashes around the boat, and a few of them were large enough to make him consider putting a line in the water. He enjoyed fishing and catching a few might add credence to his disguise.

But he was working a schedule. They'd be waiting at the dock. He'd go fishing another day. Perhaps on Lake Galich near the private home he'd be awarded for services to the party.

Another splash, this one closer than the others. He peered to the port side, trying to catch a glimpse of what had to be a monster fish. A ripple betrayed a large shape moving near the boat. He leaned in for a better look and found a tight-set pair of black eyes peering back.

They became a blur along with the rest of the great head as the alligator leapt from the water and snapped its jaws onto his shoulder. There was no possibility of fighting back as the twisting horror of teeth and scales pulled him into the lake, capsizing the boat.

The beast wasn't alone. Pushkin had found a con-

gregation of them. At least half a dozen sets of jaws took turns keeping him under, each tearing off a piece of the Russian and swimming off to keep it for themselves.

His submerged screams filled his lungs with water. Death came quickly. He drowned before he bled out.

Some of the alligators ignored Pushkin and turned their attention to everything else that fell out of the boat. They indiscriminately gnawed on his tackle box and fishing gear. The oars and extra life vests met similar fates. As did the cooler, and its contents.

The hazardous materials carrier unit was designed to float, and the reptiles felt a warm tingle coming off it. It drew them. They thought it was worth getting at, worth eating. They struck at each other to earn a chance to shake and chomp at the thing; to break it open.

At last, one succeeded. The exposed contents repelled the alligators. Instinctively, they sensed something foul about the smooth cylinder that sank so quickly.

The entire congregation fled to shore and an 85-pound rod of triple-enriched uranium dropped straight to the bottom. The current moved steadily over its mass.

A string of powerful, radioactive tri-particles traveled down the river.

Thirty minutes later, the cargo van didn't arrive at the AN1 lab as scheduled. Radio attempts to reach the van failed.

Steve Smith, Barry Johnson, the van, and the uranium were still missing later in the afternoon. Doctor Monica Sherman and her team gave up on keeping it quiet and called the Atomic Energy Commission.

The next day, U.S. Government agents found the storage building, the cargo van, and Barry Johnson's

corpse. They beat Pushkin's disposal team to the structure by ninety minutes.

Then they arrested everyone at SEFOR.

The next day, a raccoon infected with bubonic plague was found dead on the southern bank of Lake Dardanelle. The Department of Fish and Game sealed off the south side of the lake to make certain the incident was isolated.

But that story was a ruse. There was no dead raccoon, and the crew wasn't looking for other infected animals. They were actually agents recovering a ten-inch cylinder of triple-enriched uranium from the lake bottom. A covert clean-up operation followed the recovery.

For a total of 58 hours, radioactive tri-particles had flowed freely downstream.

———

Eddie Beaumont did a half jog to the indoor shoreline of the east dome. Doctor Gertrude Peterson, hip-deep in her waders, moved among the coral with a hand-held aqua-scope. "Come on, Gertie," he said. "We're due in the conference area for the morning brief."

She climbed to the shore and peeled off the waders in the changing area. Underneath, she had on shorts and a pair of deck shoes. "Feels good to get out of those. Still not used to Arkansas."

"Allergies?"

"No, it's the heat and the damp," she said, then gathered up some loose pages and her binder. She put them in a box with four sealed beakers.

"You need help?" asked Eddie.

"No thanks, I've got it." She carried the box and walked with Eddie. "Like I was saying, I went from a zero-humidity ice box to this sunbaked swamp."

"The ice box, that was with Cousteau?" asked Ed-

die, opening the door. They walked in and joined the Kincaids at the table.

"Yes, two months on the Calypso. We were following a pod of fin whales through the North Atlantic off Newfoundland. Keeping up with them was a challenge. They can do fifteen knots without even trying."

"Whales sound like the opposite of microbiology," said Mike.

"And good morning," said Evelyn.

"Yes, hello," said Peterson, arranging the contents of her box on the table. "I wasn't researching the whales directly. My part was studying their diet. Krill mostly, and in turn the krill's diet of phytoplankton."

"Looks like you brought some show-and-tell things," said Evelyn, handing out the briefs for the meeting.

"Yes," said Peterson. "But you go first."

"Okay," said Mike. "We've only got one thing we wanted to talk about. We want to be sure we stay efficient. This is a government facility and that comes with a lot of requests for forms and meetings."

"It's easy to get stuck in redundant nonsense," said Evelyn. "So, over the next week, let's check in with everyone and see if we can't eliminate a few processes out of our day-to-day."

"Now you're talking my language," said Eddie.

"Between all departments, we figure we can knock an hour or two of pointless practice out of each day," said Evelyn. "That's a whole shift over the course of a week."

"With my hours that's more like half a shift," said Eddie.

"You don't have a time card," said Mike. "You are free to come and go as you please."

"Hours mean nothing to me, Mike." Eddie pulled his hands over his heart and looked skyward. "This job is a dream I want to stay in forever. Besides, there

isn't a lot I can do with my free time here in Pope County."

"We are inside a recreation zone," said Evelyn. "People travel here from all over. Boats, fishing, hiking, the works."

"Sounds like torture to this Chicago boy," said Eddie.

"Speaking of boating," said Peterson. "I took the launch a little ways downstream at sunrise today. Maybe two miles."

That information hung in the room for a moment as Peterson handed around a data-sheet and organized her beakers.

"Why do I think this is the beginning of bad news?" said Eddie, scrutinizing the paper.

"Not bad, Chicago Boy. Just news," said Peterson. "Some of your microbial stowaways have moved along the river."

"Why did they leave the coral?" asked Evelyn. "They're linked. Symbiotic."

"I guess we can't contain a microorganism without a microscopic cage," said Mike.

"Things move, it's what they do," said Peterson. "Might have been the current, or a fish knocked them loose. Hard to say."

"Okay," said Mike. "Our stowaways are on a river tour."

Peterson raised a large beaker with small, tan slips of something clinging to the sides. "Tour's over for these guys. I brought a few of them back."

"This still sounds bad," said Eddie.

"Nothing in nature is bad. It just *is*," said Peterson. "These are flatworms from the Amazon. They hitched a ride on your corals, and they are doing what flatworms do - swimming, eating, and making more flatworms. I found these in a reed bed. All kinds of yummy treats there and every one is a new flavor.

Frog eggs, carp eggs, algae. Turns out these guys love the local cuisine. They've gone native."

"We've introduced something new to an established ecosystem," said Evelyn. "Eddie's right, this could be bad."

"Again, nature isn't bad. It just is," said Peterson. "But..."

"I knew it," said Eddie.

"There *is* a puzzle here," said Peterson, handing the beaker off to Evelyn. "This species of flatworm is supposed to be tiny. You can fit fifty on your pinkie nail."

Evelyn held the beaker at eye level. "Most of these are the same size as my pinkie nail. A few are even bigger."

"It's odd," said Peterson. "I've got more of them isolated in a table-top aquarium. I'll do some tests and figure out what makes them different."

"How far downstream do you think they've travelled?" asked Mike.

"No way to tell," said Peterson. "The farthest they can go is the Delta Basin down in Louisiana. That would take weeks, but they can't get any farther because the salt water will kill them."

"Pioneers, leaving the coral beds for a better way of life," said Eddie, trying his best to sound like a movie. "Some are doomed, some will thrive. It's a lesson from history."

"I dropped some catch-buckets two miles down river," said Peterson. "I'll check them for more specimens in a few days. It's likely some predator will develop a taste for these flatworms, then their numbers will go down. They may even be eliminated. They're the new neighbors, and the welcome committee is bound to greet them soon. And eat them soon."

6

Two days later, Evelyn didn't like what she saw in the daily reports. She went to the main lab looking for Mike. He wasn't there, but she did find Eddie. He was on the phone, and ended the call when he saw her come in.

"Odd things in this morning's numbers," said Evelyn. "Have you seen Mike? Have you seen this report?"

"I haven't looked at the reports yet," said Eddie. "That was Mike on the line. I'm supposed to find you. We're wanted in the conference area. I guess no one answered in your office."

"Because I'm here."

"Not anymore. Off we go." Eddie led her into the hall. "What's bad in the report?"

"Three more corals are showing die off," she said. "And one patch has strange outgrowths. It's sudden. And it's only the ones in the river, none of the tanks are affected."

They walked into the conference area, and found Mike seated at the table.

Albert Sawyer from the Department of the Interior paced about. Felicia Ward from the Department of

Health, Education, and Welfare sat at the table and scribbled out notes in a journal book.

A large man in a dark suit closed the doors once Evelyn and Eddie were inside. He wore an earpiece with a wire running under his coat. "Take a seat, please," said the stranger.

They did.

Sawyer addressed the stranger. "Troy, loosen up." He joined the others at the table. "Everyone, the man at the door is Troy Madden. He's with an agency I'm not supposed to mention. Say 'hello' to the nice people, Troy."

"Hello," said Troy.

An offset chorus of greetings bounced around the room.

"What's going on?" said Mike. "This morning our corals are going haywire, then you all turn up out of nowhere."

"For most of the day and part of the night yesterday," said Ward, "Albert and I were in meetings with the C.I.A., the F.B.I., the Atomic Energy Commission, and, for a few minutes over the phone, Vice President Agnew."

"Should I be here?" asked Eddie. "This sounds like I shouldn't be here."

"We've been instructed to give this information to you three and no one else. Verbally," said Sawyer. "Troy is here to make sure I get it right."

"Okay," said Evelyn. "You have the floor."

"We've had an espionage incident at the SEFOR lab, west of here," said Sawyer.

"That's Monica Sherman's outfit," said Mike. "What do you mean by 'espionage?'"

"Someone tried to steal something," said Ward. "It didn't work out for them. We've recovered the stolen article and cleaned up the area. But for three days the

river was exposed to radioactive material. We don't know yet if it's caused problems."

"We've had some irregularities with our coral beds," said Evelyn.

"Mutations, too," said Mike. "Those larger flatworms."

"Can this be related to our incident?" asked Madden.

"I'll need to run tests," said Eddie. "Look for lingering radiation."

Sawyer stood. "Do what you have too," he said. "If there's anything you need help with, call me directly."

"Albert is point on this," said Ward. "But I'm ready if you need anything from my department. I'm sorry this happened. Hope it hasn't crushed the project."

"How's Doctor Sherman?" asked Evelyn.

"Doctor Sherman is taking some time away," said Troy Madden. "Don't try to contact her, please. Communication should go through Mr. Sawyer."

"If we need to deal with issues here in the facility," said Mike, "some of our people are going to have to know some things."

"Your top-level people can hear what we've told you," said Sawyer. "Because we didn't tell you much. But use discretion, please."

After seeing the government people to their sedan, Mike and Evelyn made a straight run for Gertrude Peterson's lab and told her everything they knew about the trouble upstream.

Discreetly.

Outside, Eddie waded in river with a Geiger counter.

BRET NELSON

Discreetly.

Peterson poured through datasets in one of her many binders, tracking changes in the river-planted beds over the last week. "I'm not worried about the corals," she said. "They're resilient. The die off and odd growth we're seeing now will likely be the only trouble we have with them." She passed the binder to the Kincaids. "Check line fourteen on the day-to-day. There are slight fluctuations starting last week, and that's when the radiation was introduced, right?"

"Right," said Evelyn. "But now the radioactive source is gone."

"Then we'll see things improve quickly," said Peterson. "Clean water will bring clean food. If the algae they've cultivated is unhealthy, the coral will stop cultivating it and it will stop growing. It was too late for some, and those polyps died."

"If I'm following this," said Mike, "the ones that are alive are safe. Any irradiated algae will die and wash away, and healthful algae will grow in its place."

"Gold star, Dr. Kincaid," said Evelyn.

"Yes," said Peterson. "And I doubt the cast-off algae with cause any trouble downstream."

Eddie Beaumont came in wearing a different outfit and drying his hair with a towel. "Fell in," he said. "The radiation levels are normal. They did a good job on the clean up."

"That's nice to hear," said Evelyn. She had close eyes on twenty-three tan slips clutching to the side of a small aquarium. "Have these got any bigger?" she asked.

"Not by much," said Peterson. "Once they landed in that tank they grew by about five percent then stopped. I expect them to increase in number, though."

"We were wondering if the flatworms' anomalies

might have been a byproduct of the radiation," said Mike. "A mutation where the genetic cap on cell replication and growth was twisted."

"Or eliminated," said Eddie. "Woah. If it were eliminated, the only things restricting their size are available food and living space."

Peterson joined the others at the aquarium. "It's possible. These may have stopped growing because *this* tank supports *this* size. I'll move some of them to a larger environment and see what we get."

"Hey, when was the last time you went downstream?" asked Evelyn. "To the area where you left the catch basins?"

Everyone in the room froze.

"I haven't been at all," said Peterson. "I was going to go this afternoon."

"Oh no," said Mike. "If those flatworms carry this mutation, they might have been growing unchecked for days."

"In a big living space," said Evelyn.

"We can all fit in the launch," said Peterson. "It's the only way to get there. There isn't a road within miles of that part of the river."

———

"Good Lord, they're big as bath towels," said Evelyn.

"And they smell like gym socks," said Eddie, scrunching up his nose.

Flatworms, each about a yard square, covered the shallows in front of the launch. Many were draped over the half-submerged boulders along the shoreline. Others scooted on the bottom seeking a meal or a surface to grip. A few hundred feet ahead, the landscape formed a pinch point in the river leading to deeper, faster waters. The colony stopped there.

"For crying out loud, what are we going to do,

47

Mike?" asked Eddie. "Why aren't the flatworms in our coral beds growing this large? Weren't they irradiated? Don't they carry that mutated gene?"

"Maybe once the mutants grew large enough, they turned loose of the coral. Got swept downstream," said Mike.

"That sounds right," said Peterson. "There's a slowdown in the current here. Lots of places to stick. Lots of things to eat. It's everything they're looking for."

"We have to stop them, right here," said Evelyn. "Looks like about fifty of them give or take."

"Let's hassle a few into the launch. Get them to the lab," said Mike. "We've got to get them to the lab. See exactly what they are if we have any hope of finding a way to deal with them."

"We also have to look further downstream," said Eddie. "See if there are more."

7

They brought two flatworms back to the facility. Both survived the trip.

The small dock for the launch was out of sight of the main domes. They carried the specimens through the service entrance in laundry bags. One went to Doctor Evelyn Kincaid's biolab for dissection. The other was placed in the largest tank in Doctor Gertrude Peterson's marine lab.

Mike insisted they keep the specimens a secret from the rest of the staff until they learned more about them.

———

An hour later, Evelyn Kincaid sat at her desk, paging through the notes she'd just written, double-checking them against her reference books to make sure she spelled "Platyhelminthes" correctly.

She had.

The rimmed metal table in the center of her lab was strewn with bowls and trays holding the organs and pieces that once made up a mutant flatworm. The

dissection process had been difficult. Out of the water the worm was dead weight.

Mike and Eddie eased through the door. "Are we interrupting?" asked Mike.

"Not at all. I'm done," said Evelyn.

Mike rubbed her shoulders. "How are you holding up?"

"I'm good. But that damn thing is heavy."

Eddie looked over the remains on the table. "Ah Mom, flatworm again?" he said.

"He's a little giddy," said Mike. "Our government friends are taking Eddie on a helicopter ride in the morning."

"I'm going on recon," he said. "We're going to buzz the river from here to Little Rock. See if we can spot another colony."

"And Al wants us to keep this quiet for now," said Mike.

"No surprise there," said Evelyn.

"Troy Madden says 'hi,'" added Eddie. "I think he's a secret agent man."

"I've got a feeling we're going to see a lot of him," said Evelyn. She handed her notes to Mike. "The dissection didn't reveal any secrets. Other than the size, they are regular flatworms."

"Is that bad?" asked Mike.

"Yes," said Evelyn. "It means their numbers can grow exponentially."

"How?" asked Eddie.

"Now that you're older," said Evelyn, "we should have a talk about where flatworms come from."

"It's not the stork?" said Eddie.

"No," said Evelyn. "Flatworms are adaptive. With a pair of them, you get a clutch of fertilized eggs they lay in a mass, or they can carry them depending on which is better for their situation."

"Maybe our mutants are sterile," said Mike.

"Doubt it," said Evelyn. "The ones Gertie brought here a few days ago have already reproduced."

"Can they bud?" said Mike.

"Sadly, yes. They don't *need* a partner or eggs to reproduce. They can force buds to grow along their length and when each one is big enough, it breaks off to form a new worm. Plus, if they're in real distress, they can use transverse fission."

"Don't know that one," said Eddie.

"Half of a worm fastens to a surface and the other half keeps moving forward until the damn thing pulls apart," said Evelyn. "Each half regenerates to form a complete flatworm."

"A few species can pull themselves into several pieces and make several worms," said Doctor Peterson. The others hadn't heard her come in. She carried a new binder.

"So, if the Army gets involved, they can't use heavy ordinance," said Mike.

"Gold star, Doctor Kincaid," said Evelyn. "Blast one into a hundred pieces and you might get a hundred worms."

"Did you have any luck, Gertie?" asked Eddie.

"They are resistant to every poison we have, and we have all the poisons," she said. "The concentration needed to wipe out the colony would kill everything downstream and make the river deadly for years. Our best bet is a safer chemical approach, rather than poisons. Shock the colony with some kind of additive to the water that's harmless to the surrounding people and wildlife. Like using salt on snails."

"We know of anything like that for flatworms?" asked Mike.

"Flatworms are notorious for infesting aquariums," said Peterson. "They arrive as stowaways, like the ones on your corals."

"So how do you get rid of them?" asked Eddie.

"A mild solution of citric acid will kill them off without damaging the other fish in the tank," she said. "But I've tried every concentration and derivative of citric acid, and it doesn't have any effect on this mutant species. Their size has made their hides and digestive systems tougher."

She handed the binder to Mike. "Keep this, I've got another copy. All my results are there."

Mike paged through the binder. "This is complete. Looks like we've got a big puzzle."

Eddie used a pair of forceps to lift a scrap of flatworm from the table. "Hang on, maybe the answer is here! How did you kill this one?"

"I put a spike through its brain," said Evelyn.

"Hmm. Not easy to implement with a whole colony," said Eddie.

"Maybe, with enough people, we could gather them up," said Mike. "A lot of boats, a lot of hands. It can be done."

"It's possible," said Peterson. "You'd have to keep coming back, though. There might be new worms so small you can't see them. They will grow and reproduce. You'd have to keep monitoring until you were sure the colony was finished."

———

The next morning, a meeting was called in the courtyard at the Science Dome. The staff was made aware of the *existence* of the mutated flatworms, but not the *cause* of the mutated flatworms.

Albert Sawyer was there with two dozen recruits from the Park Rangers he trusted to keep their mouths shut. The staff at the Science Dome had signed confidentiality agreements when they were hired, so their silence was presupposed. Sawyer was adamant about keeping the lid on.

Along with the rangers, he brought a flotilla of fifteen aluminum launch boats. Mike helped organize the group, and they executed his plan of hand-gathering the colony two miles down river.

By the end of the day, all forty-three of the flatworms were hauled out of the water and brought back to the Science Dome. Several were isolated in tanks for further study. The rest were pithed and destroyed in the incinerator.

Doctor Peterson protested this. Loudly. But Sawyer insisted.

"I am under orders," he said. "This is a government facility, so you are under government jurisdiction. You keep fifteen percent of the specimens. The remainder are to be disposed of. My hands are tied."

Eddie Beaumont couldn't participate in the gathering mission because he was on his recon flight, which turned out to be more work than adventure. He spent seven hours in a Bell 204B helicopter staring through binoculars at the river below. Troy Madden sat next to him and insisted on slowly covering the same 50-mile stretch of waterway four times: east bound, west bound, then again in both directions using a crisscross pattern.

On the third pass, they found another colony. They'd missed it on the previous runs because it was huddled at a crook in the river. Eddie met with the Kincaids that evening and showed them the reconnaissance photographs.

"There," he said. "You can see them in the shallows. This area is isolated, not a road or building for miles."

"Hard to get a scale," said Evelyn. "Are these the same size as the others?"

"Bigger. Each is like a sleeping bag and there's a lot more of them this time. It's the only other colony

53

out there. We went all the way past Little Rock, over and over."

A large map occupied a table in the conference area. Mike drew a circle. "So, this is the spot?"

"Yes," said Eddie. "It's all craggy and the water is slow. It must be what they like."

"They won't like it tomorrow," said Evelyn. "As soon as you spotted this, Madden radioed his higher-ups."

"Troy Madden is a sneaky little sneak," said Eddie. "I didn't even hear him, and he was right next to me."

"He's from the Department of Sneak," said Mike. "Pretty sure he runs it. And that earpiece he wears means he's always communicating with somebody. When he told Sawyer and Ward about this second colony, the phone calls cascaded. We're out of the picture now."

"Not entirely," said Evelyn. "We're 'advisors.'"

"That's always fun," said Eddie. "It means 'advise on the best approach to the situation so we can ignore it.'"

"I don't think it will be so bad," said Mike. "The military *is* stepping in to take out this colony, but it's Anthony Corvus putting the plan together. He'll be here before breakfast."

"The General's coming?" said Eddie. "Wow, they really do want to put this to bed. Good it's Corvus, though. I trust him."

———

At dawn, Troy Madden's sedan arrived with an additional passenger, General Anthony Corvus.

The general was tall and thin. An older man. Clean shaven with his thin grey hair combed back.

After a brief walk around the complex, they entered the conference area in the main dome.

A smile crossed the general's face when he saw coffee and food laid out. Pastries, fresh eggs, and lovely ham. The fruit even looked good.

And his smile only got bigger when he spotted Doctor Evelyn Kincaid.

"Evelyn, how long has it been?" asked Corvus. "Gotta be two years, right?"

He held both her hands, and she gave him a polite peck on the cheek.

"Sounds right," she said. "Mike, have we seen the general since Nevada?"

"Hello Tony," said Mike, shaking the general's hand. "She's right, the last time we got together we were working on VELA. Spent that spring in a Nevada bunker. Lovely time."

"Let's hope this project won't take quite so long," said Corvus, eyeing the food. "Are those goodies for everyone?"

Plates and coffee cups were filled. Seats were taken. The general gave a nod to Eddie Beaumont, who in turn introduced him to Doctor Gertrude Peterson.

Troy Madden stood at the door.

"All right," said Corvus. "Let's hear about these flatworms of yours."

Mike and Evelyn Kincaid did most of the talking. Eddie Beaumont passed the general images and graphs. Gertrude Peterson filled in blanks on the creatures' biology. She didn't like seeing them wiped out but understood they were an invasive species. Better to keep them in the lab, and she had enough specimens to keep her busy studying them for years.

Since the incinerator made short work of disposing of them, the general had a flamethrower unit on standby.

"Our best bet is the National Guard right here in Arkansas," said Corvus. He pulled some large-format operations documents out of his attaché case. "They're in close proximity to the river. Good people, too. For starters, we've got Major Paul Ryder. Sharp mind on him. Strategic thinker. If we give him a task, he'll pull it off."

"It's your call, General," said Mike.

"All right," said Corvus. "Under him, there's Sergeant Arthur Gasparo. Ryder will run the operations; Gasparo will lead the front-line unit."

"Artie's out here?" said Eddie. "He's great."

"When did you meet Gasparo?" asked Corvus.

"He was on the field tests for our P-9 wind screens," said Eddie. "You remember Evelyn, at that English base outside of Dorset."

"Oh yes," said Evelyn. "He had those exercises running like clockwork."

"Manufacturing side was a nightmare, though," said Mike. "Teams on two continents with half the engineers on standard and the other half on metric."

The room fell silent as everyone waited politely for Mike Kincaid to finish his story.

"... and that doesn't have anything to do with this," he said. "Go on, General."

"With Ryder and Gasparo, I have a high level of confidence for our success," said Corvus. "By now, they should have gathered their personnel and gear. But this being the National Guard, I've got to get the governor on board. Once he gives the go ahead, we can get this squad to the site in two hours."

"Governor Rockefeller is a fan of our work," said Evelyn. "It's why the Science Dome landed in Arkansas."

"But he's not going to be happy about mutant worms clogging up his major waterways," said Corvus.

"Won't he be happy to get rid of them?" asked Eddie. "I mean, he can't blame us for this. He knows about the nuclear spy theft, right?"

"Do you?" asked Troy Madden.

"Um... maybe?" said Eddie, finding a point of interest in his coffee cup.

"I get it," said Corvus. "These flatworm mutations are a byproduct of the mess at SEFOR. This is part of the ongoing cleanup." He walked to table with the large map. "The area you've got circled is still the best place for our unit to make contact, right?"

"Yes," said Mike. "South of Easterwood Point Road in Faulkner County. It's where they've decided to stay. The river runs shallow and slow there."

"That's about thirty miles away," said Corvus. "How long did it take them to get there?"

"Three days," said Evelyn.

"All right, there's a lot to coordinate," said Corvus. "If you are all on board with this, I'll acquire clearance to commence the operation."

The general didn't need to ask anyone if it was all right to move forward, but he wanted to hear if there was any reason *not* to proceed.

There wasn't.

"Would it help if I was on the call with the governor?" asked Mike.

"No need," said Corvus. "I'm calling the president. He'll call the governor."

8

Two Army transport trucks and a half-track loaded with gear turned off Easterwood Point Road and headed cross-country toward the river. "There," said Major Paul Ryder, riding shotgun in the lead truck. "That hill with the lone pine on top. That's where we'll set up observation and comms. River's right below."

"Sir, yes Sir," said Private Taylor. He turned the truck toward the hill and reached out the window, waving the others to follow.

Ryder looked skyward through his window. "Any word on my support chopper?"

"We're supposed to have a Kiowa with us, Sir, but they got delayed. They'll be here as soon as they can."

"Dammit."

In the next truck, Private Gil Williams drove while his squad leader, Sergeant Arthur Gasparo, paged through the mission brief in the passenger seat.

"If you don't mind me asking, Sarge," said Williams, "Are we really being deployed against worms?"

"Can confirm," said Gasparo. He slid open the

window behind him and called to the men riding benches in the back. "Looks like we're in pest control, gentlemen." That got a laugh all around. "But take this seriously. These are mutated creatures. Used to be tiny flatworms but somehow they've grown to eight feet or so. Sounds like something out of a drive-in double-feature, but it's real. There's hundreds of them, and they've got to be stopped before they reach the dams and bridges east of here. No one has seen anything like this before."

"So, they called in the best!" shouted Williams.

All the men hollered in chorus, "The Arkansas Brigade!"

———

The conference area of the main dome had become the center of operations for the flatworm issue. Soldiers kept arriving, and with them came maps of varied size and detail. They hung all over the walls alongside note-covered chalkboards and cork-boards strewn with documents, photos, and strings. A top-of-the-line radio comm station was powered up and tested in less than half an hour, and that included erecting a twenty-foot aerial on the domed roof.

At the center of the military's efficiency whirlpool sat Michael Kincaid. He was the only "advisor" left in the room and he didn't have anything to do. The others had gone to their respective labs, mostly because they felt in the way.

General Corvus came in and scanned the faces, looking for Doctor Kincaid. "Hell's monkeys! Where did all these people come from?" he muttered. Then he spotted Mike and joined him at the table.

"The governor authorized The Arkansas Brigade to help us stop the beasts' progress," said Corvus.

"They are en route, arriving at the river before lunchtime."

"Arkansas Brigade?" said Doctor Kincaid.

"That's the Army National Guard. Specifically, the First Battalion, 206th Field Artillery Regiment," said the general. "The 206th is an element of the 39th Infantry Brigade Combat Team. I can step you through all the designations, but we'll get in the weeds pretty quick."

"That's not necessary, thank you," said Mike.

Gertrude Peterson's lab housed the biggest tank in the complex. Eddie called it "The Tank of Days," because it took two days to fill it. Each wall was twenty feet high and thirty feet wide. It gave Peterson's desk quite a backdrop.

When Evelyn arrived to discuss the current Ph readings in the coral beds, she took little notice of Doctor Peterson. All she saw was the ten-foot flatworm in The Tank of Days.

"Good morning," said Peterson.

"Good morning," said Evelyn, eyes locked on the worm. "Is that alive?"

Gertrude Peterson glanced over her shoulder then returned to writing up her notes. "Yes," she said. "Yes it is."

"Is that a manta ray?" asked Evelyn.

"No, it is not."

"Is that an Oldsmobile?" asked Evelyn.

"No," said Peterson, laughing. She joined Evelyn on the other side of her desk for a better look at the flatworm. "It is a Planaria Giganticus. Best name I could come up with, anyway. Maybe we can think of something better."

"Giganticus... I like it a lot, it's on point. I'll start using it everywhere and tell Mike to do the same."

"This is the biggest tank, and the flatworm grew to fit." She handed a page of notes to Evelyn. "They definitely expand to their environments. In beakers, they're still as big as your pinky nail. The ones in the thirty-gallon aquariums are like potato chips. Then, you've got this bruiser."

———

The trucks pitched and splashed through deep mud that shouldn't have been there.

"What the hell?" said Major Ryder.

"Water patches all along here, Sir," said Private Taylor. "Looks like the river breached its banks."

"Didn't expect that. And I hate surprises. And where's my damn chopper?"

The trucks crested the rise and stopped on the hilltop with the lone pine. Everyone got out and looked down on the gray mass of flatworms. It stretched for a mile. Each soldier wore waders. At this time of year, the river should have been knee-high.

It was barely six inches deep.

What used to be the river had been replaced by mounds of flatworms. They were bigger than reported. Each could easily cover a school bus.

They were piled on top of one another. Hundreds of them. Maybe thousands, it was hard to tell as they were layered twenty feet high in places. Shifting constantly, one heap spilling over to form two others.

The major bellowed loud enough for all to hear. "Don't stand there staring all slack-jawed, it's only a goddamn herd of giant flatworms. We are on the clock, people! Unload that gear and get your shit together. Move!"

The men got to work. Ryder jogged to his truck, leaned into the cabin, and switched on the radio.

"Base, come in Base," he said, squeezing the handset. "This is Batt One, Actual. Do you copy? Over."

Back in the dome, General Anthony Corvus dismissed the radio operator and took his seat. Then he pressed the talk button on the microphone and locked it open. Michael Kincaid stood near the radio's speaker.

"We've got you, Batt One. This is General Corvus. You're on a speaker, so Doctor Kincaid can hear you, too. Over."

"All right, General. Here's the latest," said Ryder. "We have reached the coordinates, two and a quarter miles south of Easterwood Point Road. Doctor Kincaid, be aware - the whole area is overrun with these flatworms of yours. Near as we can guess, they are displacing the river. Water level is low, less than a foot, and the surrounding landscape is soaked. Over."

Mike leaned into the microphone. "Can you say that again? I want to be sure I've heard it correctly." He waited for a response, but none came. The general spoke for him.

"Over," said Corvus.

Private Williams ran up and handed a set of field glasses to Major Ryder. "They're moving, Sir," he said.

"Hang on, Base. New information coming in. Break."

Through the field glasses, the major watched a mass of flatworms slide off a particularly tall pile a quarter mile away. They skimmed along on top of the others and came to rest forming a new front. In moments, the creatures had shifted several yards closer to Little Rock.

The major called to Sergeant Gasparo. "Artie, have your boys get those flamethrowers strapped on. Let's

get the heat going and drive these bastards back." He returned his attention to the handset. "Base, this is Batt One, Actual. Do you copy? Over."

"We're here," said Mike. "Um, over."

"Your briefing was inaccurate, Doctor Kincaid. Each creature looks a little shy of a ten yards wide. And they are stacked up in twenty-foot piles. And where's my recon chopper? Over."

"Helo is en route from Fort Chaffee," said Corvus. "Sorry, Paul. Some brass needed transport this morning and you got bumped. Over."

Ryder shook his head. "Guess your worms aren't a priority. Over."

"Begging your pardon, Major, I want to be sure about something," said Mike. "Each specimen is ten yards - thirty feet across. Did I hear you right? Over."

"That's right. We're sending a flamethrower unit in now. Over."

"All right," said Mike. "Thank you Major Ryder. Over."

"Just another day at the office. Batt One out." Major Ryder tossed the handset into the truck and walked ten steps to the operations tent, a three-sided affair the men had erected while he was on the horn.

The M9 flamethrower unit, led by Sergeant Gasparo, moved down the hill to their positions. They formed a line in the river fifty yards from the eastern edge of the flatworm colony, standing between it and the city of Little Rock forty miles away. The water only came up to their ankles. The worms had formed a loose dam.

Gasparo spoke into his walkie talkie. "Major Ryder, are you on this channel? Over."

In the tent, one of the men handed Ryder a walkie. "I've got you, Artie," he said. "I can see you through the field glasses. You about ready? Over."

"Stinks to high heaven down here," he said. "It's like they're all sweating cabbage. Over."

"I'll report it to the whiz-kids back at the Science Dome. Over." said Ryder.

"Right," said Gasparo. "We're in position. Waiting for the word. Over."

"Given," said Ryder. "It's your show, Sergeant. Over and out."

Gasparo handed the walkie talkie to Private Williams, his support, who strapped it around his shoulder. Then Gasparo addressed the unit. "All right, firebugs. Keep aware of each other and mind your spacing. Only burn the worms, right? Now, get hot!"

In near perfect sync, the men slapped the levers on their flamethrowers that lit the small torch at the edge of the nozzle.

"And open 'em up!" hollered Gasparo. "Make the wall!"

Each guardsman pulled the handle tight, and a column of flame leapt from their weapons. With a few adjustments in angle and stance, the individual streams of fire became an interconnected maelstrom thirty-five yards in front of the men.

"Forward!" called Sergeant Gasparo. In unison, they took two careful steps forward. bringing the wall of flame closer to the worm colony.

"They don't like it, Sir," said Private Williams, spotting through his binoculars. "Flames aren't even touching them yet and they're already flinching."

He was right. Those closest to the fire wall, on the periphery of the colony, recoiled. They pulled back as their edges singed.

"Advance!" called Sergeant Gasparo. The unit cut their weapons, stepped forward five yards into new positions, and resumed firing.

The scorched worms retreated further, scooting

underneath the ones stacked behind them. That brought a fresh group of the beasts in line with the flames, replacing their charred brethren.

"Advance!" called Sergeant Gasparo. The unit cut their weapons, stepped forward five yards into new positions, and resumed firing.

And again, the leading row of creatures tucked themselves under the pile. Fresh ones tumbled over to replace them. They, in turn, blistered from the heat and forced their way beneath the others.

Major Ryder surveyed the scene below through his field glasses and hollered to the radio operator in the tent. "Barnes, send word to the base. Tell them it's working; the slimy shits hate the flamethrowers. They're backing away."

"Calling now, Sir," said Barnes.

"And tell Doctor Kincaid these things smell lousy."

"Smell lousy," echoed Barnes. "Yes, Sir."

As the cycle of burning continued, the flatworm landscape changed. The worms scuttling over the top of the colony increased in number. Instinct drew them toward their wounded brethren, a source of proteins. More of them were piling up.

"Advance!" called Sergeant Gasparo. The unit cut their weapons, stepped forward five yards into new positions, and resumed firing.

"There's an awful lot of them on top, Sir," said Private Williams, scanning with his binoculars. The men holding the flamethrower line saw only fire.

Ryder saw trouble through his field glasses. He grabbed his walkie.

"Gasparo! Retreat! Get back! The damn things are too high, they're going to fall!"

Too late. The actions of the monster flatworms moving underneath and over each other formed a wave, and it crested at fifty feet. All at once, hundreds

of the mutations fell. The colony thundered outward in all directions, stopping ten yards from the observation tent on the hill.

There was no sign of the flamethrower unit. Or Sergeant Gasparo. Or Private Williams. No sign of any wounded worms, either. Everything got buried under fresh layers of giant writhing creatures.

After all that effort, the only change in the colony was its position, now two hundred yards past where The Arkansas Brigade tried to stop it.

Major Ryder got on the radio. He spoke slowly, with a shake in his voice. "Base, this is Batt One, Actual. Mission failure, repeat, mission failure. Sergeant Gasparo, Private Williams, and the entire flamethrower unit are lost. Time to trigger Plan 470. Is that understood? Over."

"Understood. Plan 470 in effect," said General Corvus. "I'm sorry, Paul. Over."

"One more thing, I think they'll make Little Rock sooner than you've estimated. Doctor Kincaid, you need to get your people out here to monitor these things. You copy? Over."

"Yes," said Mike. "Yes, I'll get out there with a team right away."

"Thank you Major," said Corvus. "Over and out."

Ryder dropped the handset and looked out over the worms. "You were right, Artie," he whispered. "They stink like hell."

He spun around to his troops. "Sergeant Barnes, pick four men to load this gear onto the half-track. The rest of you, get into the other trucks - now. Taylor, you drive lead. Billings, Sands, you drive the trucks. Let's move."

Everyone got to work. Taylor carried gear but stopped to talk with the major. "Where are we headed, Sir?" he asked.

"Back to camp. Got to retool," said Ryder.

"For what, Sir?"

"Plan 470," said the major. "Evacuating Little Rock."

"Should any of us stay here to monitor these flat-worms?" asked Taylor.

"No need," said Ryder, looking skyward. "Here comes the goddamn recon helicopter."

9

The chopper spent three hours gathering data and images. They radioed information to Michael Kincaid and General Corvus at the Science Dome.

The colony now covered 1.7 miles, favoring the riverbanks and avoiding the stronger current in the center. Each flatworm was roughly eleven yards square. Film shot by the recon team documented the flatworms' reproduction via budding. It took 30 minutes from the time growths appeared on a worm's edge for those growths to break free as new worms. Each of those new flatworms took another thirty minutes to grow to the size of their parent. Only about ten percent of the specimens were budding.

The flatworms progressed half a mile east during the recon helicopter's survey. The western edge of the colony hadn't changed position, which meant the colony wasn't moving.

It was expanding.

"You know you have to get out there, right?" said Corvus.

"Of course," said Mike.

"Madden is hassling jeeps and drivers for you. What kind of gear do you need?"

"Eddie's already on that," said Mike. "He's got people gathering survey tools, video equipment, a couple of generators, and a travel lab so we can process samples in the field."

The general tapped the shoulder of one of the soldiers hovering over the map table.

"Private Dennings," he said. "Go and find Eddie Beaumont. Figure out how big a footprint his team is going to have then get enough tents and canopies on the trucks to house them. Tables and chairs, too. And a radio, with an operator."

"Sir, yes Sir," said Dennings, scratching out notes on a pad. "Should I put together a crew for set up and tear down as well?"

"Yes. Good thinking, Private," said Corvus. "I've got a feeling this circus is going to move around a lot. Off you go."

Dennings headed out, passing Gertrude Peterson and Evelyn Kincaid trying to get in. The soldier on the door blocked their way. "No, I don't have a *group access lanyard*. What is that anyway?" asked Peterson.

"Those two can come and go as they please," said Corvus. The soldier stood aside.

"We only just got word," said Evelyn. "I so sorry, Tony."

"Mission failure is always possible," said Corvus. "But hell's monkeys, I didn't expect fatalities. Got to get a new plan together. Quick."

"I'm heading to the site with Eddie and his team," said Mike. "Evelyn, can you stay by the radio with the general?"

"Of course. You be careful," said Evelyn.

"I will," said Mike. "Gertie, please keep working with the specimens in your lab. There's got to be something we can use to stop these things."

"I've had a sideways thought," said Peterson. "If radiation started this, could radiation end it?"

"Small problem there," said Corvus. "They won't let us irradiate Arkansas."

"No one is suggesting that," said Evelyn. "Well, Troy Madden might."

"There are all kinds of radiation," said Peterson. "Harmless atmospheric waves surround us all the time, like light and radio. A concentration of such a wave is something this species hasn't been exposed to before. And the local flora and fauna shouldn't be affected at all."

"Yes," said Mike. "Concentrating omnipresent energy. It's definitely worth looking at."

"Glad you're here, Doctor Peterson," said Evelyn.

"Glad to be here. I'll start with different spectrums of light. Look for sensitivities," said Peterson, and she left for her lab.

"Mike, Evelyn, can you get a look at this map?" asked Corvus. He introduced a new arrival who carried a fine leather case full of drafting and navigation tools. "This is Corporal Simms, an excellent cartographer."

Introductory greetings passed around the table.

"I need to tell Simms where these flatworms might show up next."

"That's difficult to say," said Mike.

"Then guess. I've got four recon choppers fueling up. They need coordinates. And this big map is going to be our central view of reality until this whole thing is over."

"We don't guess," said Evelyn. "We need time to take what facts we have and come up with an accurate hypothesis."

"We call that a *good* guess," said Corvus. "You can call it whatever you want but do it. Hypothesize. Postulate. Get out a Ouija board, if need be. We have to get marks on this map right now."

"General, please..." said Mike.

"No," said Corvus. He took a step back and spoke loud enough for the room to hear. "Every one of you needs to have a bigger sense of urgency. There's too much to do, too much at stake. We need to set up positions now if we've got any hope of helping people. We have to mobilize first aid battalions and coordinate with the Red Cross to create evacuation centers.

"But that's only half of it. Our troops must get ahead of those flatworms so we can be ready and waiting when they show up. We've got to be at the points on the river where these slimy bastards haven't got to yet - but will."

He put his arms around the Kincaids' shoulders. "So, bash those eggheads of yours together into a big, thinky omelet. Then tell me where to put our resources."

"But what if we're wrong?" asked Mike.

"No need to worry about that," said Corvus. "You're already wrong – about their size. Now you're free to screw up like the rest of us."

———

The caravan hauling Dr. Michael Kincaid, his team, and their gear grew to more than a dozen vehicles. He wondered if it was too much, but General Corvus made it clear that bigger was better, as this collection was going to become a mobile command center. Traveling until these incidents with the flatworms concluded.

When they arrived at the colony's location in Faulkner County, Kincaid was surprised to find Troy Madden already there, along with a full battalion of National Guard personnel. Two flamethrower units and support staff along with enough tents and RVs to make it look like they'd had a week to dig in.

All the activity failed to distract Michael Kincaid

from the flatworms. Like giant dumplings in a bowl, they shifted and writhed in the river below.

"The eastern edge is right past this turn, Mike." The voice snapped Kincaid out of the buzzing of theories in his head. It was Eddie Beaumont, peering through binoculars. How long had he been standing there? "I'll get our gear set up about 100 yards past the colony's eastern edge," he said.

"Yes," said Kincaid. "Thank you, Eddie. I'm going to check in with Madden. I'll walk to you after, take a good look at these things on the way."

Beaumont was already running back to the trucks. "Got it. See you in a few," he called. Kincaid pulled a small notebook from his pocket and scribbled observations until a new voice derailed his thoughts again.

"We're going to try the flamethrowers again," said Madden. "This time, the squads will hold positions up here, where the bank is higher than the flatworms. They won't be overrun this time."

"Okay," said Kincaid. He pocketed his notebook. "How did you get all this set up so quickly?"

"This is the backup squad. They were already en route in case something went wrong with the initial assault." Madden pointed to a large, cube-shaped man barking orders at the soldiers darting around him. "That's Major Charles Boreland. He's in charge of these people."

"Are you in charge of him?" asked Kincaid.

"I advise him."

"And he takes your advice?"

"Every time."

"Where's Ryder? The one from this morning?"

"He's setting up evacuation protocols. Done it before and he's very good at it." Madden gave a nod to several people trying to get his attention. "I'm glad you're here, Doctor. How long do you think it will take your people to stage their gear?"

"I'm joining them now," said Kincaid. "Shouldn't be more than an hour. But don't wait for us. If you're ready to try something, do it."

"The squad will be ready at the colony's eastern front in 30 minutes. If this approach is ineffective, we'll consider bigger ordinance. Like napalm."

"The collateral damage will be catastrophic!" said Kincaid. "You can't actually be considering napalm, can you?"

"*Everything* is up for consideration. It may seem like an impossible choice now, but who knows what's coming? You?"

Kincaid looked out over the ever-shifting topography of giant flatworms. "Probably not. I sure didn't see this coming."

"We'll keep our communication lines efficient and our recon up-to-date," said Madden. "If we reach a point where the collateral damage from the ordinance is modest compared to the direct damage from these monsters, well that's that. The napalm becomes viable."

Madden put his hand on Kincaid's shoulder. "It's only math. You understand math don't you, Doctor?"

———

Two flamethrower units this time, one on either side of the river. Each at an elevation well above the worm colony. Major Boreland fired a flare pistol, signaling each soldier to start raining fire on the worms below.

As before, the creatures thrashed in the flames and struggled under the worms behind them. This exposed new beasts to the fire, and in turn they fought their way through the others to escape the blaze.

Half the National Guard units tried concentrating their fire on a single area. The rest swept wider. In either case, the burning creatures burrowed under the

layers of unscorched flatworms, and the colony expanded outward. There were no gains made against the unyielding mass of mindless creatures.

A few of the flatworms were killed. They didn't get away from the fires quickly enough. But in their death throes, they shook and twisted and forced themselves to bud. For every worm the flamethrower units managed to destroy, five new ones were brought into being. That took napalm off the table.

Kincaid and Madden returned to the Science Dome. Eddie Beaumont stayed with the team to monitor the worms' progress. General Corvus was briefed.

"We've got to talk to the press, get in front of this," said Corvus. "Hell's monkeys, what are we going to tell them?"

"The truth might be a good idea," said Evelyn.

"Bad idea," said Madden. "We can't have people think Arkansas Nuclear One is dangerous. We can't have them think it's easy for spies to steal our radioactive material. We can't have them think we're losing this fight."

"I get it," said Mike. "You can't have them think."

"That's not what he meant," said Corvus.

Mike pinned the latest photos to the status board. "Well, you had all better figure out what you're going to say. Because monsters are coming to Little Rock. Two, maybe three days at the latest. But they are coming, and the people have to evacuate."

"We've already called a press conference," said Madden. "The governor will deliver the message. He'll stick to the prepared text and the press will be satisfied."

"I don't see how," said Mike.

"You don't need to. Just figure out how to end this," said Madden. "Let us know what you need. That's your part. Let the people who tell the story do their part."

———

Later that afternoon, Eddie tuned the television set in the conference area to see the governor meet the press. Everyone stopped working to watch as Governor Winthrop Rockefeller laid out the situation to the reporters: Large animals were clogging the Arkansas River, and they were a mystery.

"It's an as-yet undiscovered species," he said, pointing to a large image of the flatworm colony behind him. "They are resistant to everything we've thrown at them. They aren't aggressive, they don't attack people. At the same time, their size and rate of reproduction makes them a threat."

"Where have these creatures come from?" asked a reporter.

"We aren't sure," said Rockefeller. "We'll find answers to questions about their origins later. The questions we need to answer now are 'where are they going?' and 'how do we stop them?'"

A series of reconnaissance photos scrolled by the screen. "An aerial survey team working the river spotted them and took these photos. As you can see, they can easily be mistaken for boulders. But if you zoom in, you can see the shapes are organic. And there are a lot of them. Hundreds."

Another reporter raised her hand. "Can't you call an exterminator?" she asked. That got laughs from her colleagues.

"Believe me, we've made many attempts to exterminate them," said Rockefeller. "So far, we haven't found a way to stop them without destroying everything else around them. Until we do, they will likely clog our waterways and cause some flooding."

The images changed from shots of the flatworms to shots of the Science Dome complex. "There is

something in our favor. The newly christened U.S. Science Dome right here in Arkansas."

Whistles and cheers went around the room. Michael Kincaid buried his head in his hands. "For crying out loud," he said. His photo filled the television monitor.

"That means we have access to the top scientific minds in the world," said Rockefeller, "and they are already working with the government and the National Guard to stop these creatures." Michael Kincaid got applause from all those around him.

The governor wrapped his message up as phone numbers and addresses of evacuation centers popped on and off the screen. "So, I am announcing, out of an abundance of caution, the evacuation of parts of Little Rock.

Troy Madden turned off the set and everyone returned to their work. Michael Kincaid approached him.

"They just accepted it," he said. "I can't believe what I saw. The reporters, they didn't question anything. They wrote it all down like kids in a classroom."

"When the subject is this fantastic, they don't know what questions to ask," said Madden. "Afraid they'll sound foolish. Then again, all they really want is a good headline. A strong lead story for the evening news. Today, we gave them a doozy, and that's enough. For now, anyway."

———

"Near as we can tell, the colony is nine layers thick," said Eddie. He spoke into a handset in the radio tent, flipping through his notes. He was following the colony as it moved east. "We can't get very close. The

air is terrible and the way they move is unpredictable. You might get crushed before you know it. Over."

Mike Kincaid and General Corvus were huddled at the radio in the Science Dome. "Evacuations are underway," said Corvus. "That's all going well."

"Can you get a gage on their speed? Their direction? Over," said Mike.

"They travel by spreading out. They pile up and fall over, so there isn't a steady rate of speed," said Eddie. "That said, I'm certain the colony will reach Little Rock by morning. Here's something else we've seen a few times, if the water breaches the banks they move into the floodwaters. So far, the flamethrowers have kept those branches from spreading. They can herd them back toward the river so far. Over."

"Given time, could they starve themselves out?" asked Mike.

"We are pretty certain they are eating each other. Over."

"So how are their numbers not shrinking?" asked Corvus.

"Their numbers are going down, but colony's mass is increasing," said Eddie. "The larger ones eat a lot of the smaller ones, then the larger ones reproduce. You end up with fewer worms, but they are much bigger. The cycle of reproduction creates more giants. It's a loss in numbers, but a net gain in mass. Over."

"I hate math," said Corvus. "And worms."

———

Little Rock was prone to flooding and the population knew what to do when the warnings were sounded. Most people paid attention to the evacuation orders.

Among the few who didn't was Terrence Williamson, a freelance photographer with two Pulitzers on his shelf back home. He was here doing a

photo essay on the recently-opened Arkansas River Navigation System, a modern marvel that promised to move millions of tons of cargo annually.

But today, it was clogged with tons of flatworms. And Terrence Williamson shot roll after roll of them, and the massive evacuation effort. He'd make a fortune with these pictures.

When there were enough beasts piled up for the river to breach the banks, they followed the water into the city. Williamson followed the action. Each image was better than the last as the flatworms piled all over Capital Avenue, heading downtown. Some gripped the sides of buildings. If you hadn't evacuated, you'd see nothing out the windows but writhing worm skin from street level to the second floor.

Half a mile away, the pressure in the flatworm colony built up and a large cluster of the beasts lurched forward. The enormous, foul wave of flatworms rolled all the way to the group on Capital Avenue. Only one minute before, they were at the end of the block. Now, filthy water moved past Williamson's ankles, and a thirty-foot wall of the ghastly things was getting too close.

The mound of creatures tilted toward him. The sound of heaving muscles and the wet slaps of worm skin drowned out everything else. Williamson turned and ran.

Warm water splashed his back as the first worms fell. He didn't look behind. He ran the fastest sprint he'd ever managed.

It didn't matter.

He landed on his stomach as a massive worm slid over him. The weight doubled when another fell on top of that one. His ribs bent. His lungs expelled air, but he couldn't draw any back in.

Something tugged his right ankle. He couldn't move and something had his ankle. Pulsating and

pulling, in a few seconds it was up to his knee and his foot got crushed. He couldn't cry out. There wasn't any breath.

He tried to shift his arms, hoping to claw his way forward because his leg was getting drawn into the mouth. Another pulsation yanked him in past his waist. His left leg, outside the maw, snapped clean at the hip joint.

Williamson blacked out. Eight seconds later, he'd been devoured completely.

———

Each afternoon, the south patio of the Hotel Conde de Villanueva in Havana was populated by old Russian men. They sat at small tables in pairs, sipping vodka and playing nardy. Most conversations were whispered. If such conversations were overheard, the listener did their best to forget them immediately.

This afternoon, one such conversation took place between Mishka Pavel, a top KGB operative, and Kosta Ilin, the only Russian board member of the newly formed World Health Organization.

Pavel had just rolled a doublet.

"Shame you can't use them," said Ilin. "I have you blocked."

"I can use one. It is all I need to get this little fellow home." Pavel moved his piece then scooped the dice into the cup and passed it to Ilan. His voice went quieter after a puff of his cigar. "From what I've been hearing, the Americans are in trouble, yes? It's as if these flatworms are working for us."

Ilin rattled the cup. "Anything is possible," he said. The dice clattered onto the board, and he moved his pieces.

"I wonder," said Pavel. "Can we acquire one for study? Perhaps learn to control them."

The dice were gathered once again, and Ilin passed the cup. "We have an agent in a high-ranking position on the U.S. science team," he said. "In the American lab, using American equipment, our agent is getting closer to a solution each day. And when a method to dominate the flatworms is discovered, the Americans will not own it. They will not control it. *We* will."

The cup shook and the dice fell to the board again. Mishka Pavel had thrown another doublet.

10

Troy Madden held his earpiece tight, nodding. "Got it," he said to no one in the room. "Thank you."

He crossed the conference area to the map where General Corvus and Corporal Simms plotted the colony's next move. "Excellent news," said Madden. "We've evacuated every population center from the colony's current location to the Mississippi River. Patrols are still moving door-to-door, but so far they haven't found many hold outs.

"Good," said Corvus. "Dennings!"

The private appeared. "Yes, Sir?"

"Get on the horn and make sure the evacuation centers are well staffed. See that the National Guard backs up the Red Cross any way they can."

"Sir, yes Sir." The private ran for the radio.

"The colony covers fifty miles, all the way from Faulkner County to Pastoria," said Simms. "Now we have to make sure the evacuees have homes to come back to. How long before these things are big enough to knock over a house?"

"The way they pile up, it's possible now," said Corvus. "The weight of hundreds of them will de-

stroy property. So will the floods. We have to stay focused on one thing - killing them."

"The Kincaids have been working with Doctor Peterson on that transmitter," said Madden. "They're making progress. Found a radio frequency that kills the smaller ones. Given another day or two working with different transmitter technologies, we should see a full-size prototype. It should at least repel and at best destroy the beasts, regardless of their size."

"Got it," said Corvus. "Dennings!"

He ran from the radio. "Sir, yes Sir?"

"How quickly can we get these transmitters deployed at scale?"

"As long as the design doesn't veer too far from what we've been given, you'll have thirty on the first day," said Dennings. "We've got all our builders on standby to fabricate them. They fit the pedestal mount for a Browning .50 caliber. Makes deployment simple. Jeeps and choppers won't need any custom parts, and they should even work on a tripod with infantry."

Troy Madden stared at the map. "What if we let them reach the Mississippi?"

"You can't be serious," said Corvus.

"Hear me out. These things can't live in the salt water, and once they get to the Mississippi the current will turn them south. When they reach the delta, they die. Then maybe we can herd the rest into the gulf."

"That's a 250-mile wall of monsters," said Simms. "And along the way, we've lost Vicksburg, Baton Rouge, who knows how many other cities."

"I understand we need to consider everything as a possibility," said Corvus. "But hell's monkeys, we can't let it come to that."

———

Most of the people who lived near the river evacuated.

A few did not.

His position with Morgan Stanley Investments meant Daniel Howard could afford anything he liked, and he liked living by the river. He liked the huge plot of land he'd bought on the banks and the enormous home he had custom built for himself, his young wife, and their two boys.

High fences and thick stands of trees isolated the mansion from the neighboring properties. These weren't needed, as privacy was guaranteed. There were no neighbors. Howard was the only person in the county who had enough money to build here.

The custom features of this new, ultramodern home in old-world Arkansas included a state-of-the-art electronic security system, a private dock, and a large-capacity floor safe.

But the most expensive part of the mansion was a secret known only to the family and the construction company that built it. A bunker.

When the cold war got hot and the missiles started sailing, Howard planned on his family keeping safe underground. Waiting out the half-life in comfort. The bunker had independent power generators, two years' worth of food, access to a fresh water well, and an assortment of amenities that put the best hotels to shame.

But as things turned out, it wasn't the threat of nuclear war that sent Daniel Howard and his family into their concrete pied-à-terre. It was a gathering of giant flatworms moving up the river along the east side of his property. He'd tried to get straight answers about the dangers this slimy, smelly threat posed, but no one from the police department or the council offices or the state house had anything useful to say.

So, he thought it best to hunker down until the Army got everything dealt with.

He called his mother in Bentonville and invited her to join them. She told him the whole thing was silly. "You've got enough money to leave if you're nervous about those animals," she said. "Go to the Carolinas, to the coast until this is over. Have some fun on the shore with the kids. I'll join you there, but I will not sit in a hole in the ground with you."

"But Mother, I built this bunker, so we don't have to leave. It's nice, like another room in the house."

"I can hear your tone," she said. "Stubborn, like your father, rest his soul. There's no talking to you out of this, is there?"

"No. Those things will reach our dock tonight. The evacuation orders have already gone out. We're going to stay under until we get the all clear."

"Well, a few days of it might be fun for the kids. But do come up into the sunshine now and then. It's not healthy for them to live like a bunch of gophers."

"There's a separate phone line," he said. "Let me give you the number, I want you to call if you change your mind."

After he'd finished failing to convince his mother to join him, Daniel Howard sealed up his grand home. Waterproof doors and windows to keep his valuables safe from flooding. Electrified security gates and fencing to keep his valuables safe from looters.

With everything secured, he took his family underground.

As predicted, the flatworm colony extended to Daniel Howard's property that evening. They were stacked high enough to push over the power lines near his private dock.

The heaps of flatworms spilled over the formerly-electrified fence and onto the eastern section of his land. Seven of the beasts blundered over the gener-

ator station. Each was larger than Howard's carport, weighing tons. The generators didn't stand a chance.

When the bunker went dark, Daniel Howard tried to keep his family calm. His battery-powered back-up lighting kicked on and he tried to operate the manual cranks to open the doors.

They were blocked by a pile of flatworms eleven layers thick. The same beasts choked the fresh air system. When his wife said water was getting in, Daniel Howard told her to shut up because leaks were impossible.

But she was right. Puddles were forming. And the phone didn't work. And what little new air came through the bending doors was noxious, thick and damp with the worm's reek.

Daniel Howard and his family fought each other to be nearest the doors and that trickle of foul air until they choked to death.

———

Private Dennings handed papers off to General Corvus. He laid them out and called the Kincaids over.

"Gather up you two," he said. "I want you to see this. We've got Czech hedgehogs piling up along the river. Miles of them."

"A Czech what?" asked Mike.

"Hedgehog. It's a tank obstacle," said Evelyn.

"Right," said Corvus. "They look like the jacks kids play with, but they're made of eight-foot steel pieces. We think if a flatworm rubs up against them they'll turn away. If so, we can use them to protect the population centers. We've set them up here, on the south side of the river by Pine Bluff."

"That sounds easier to coordinate than flamethrowers," said Mike.

"Agreed," said Corvus. "But we still need something to kill them. Obstacles won't matter once the worms get big enough to ignore them."

The idea worked. The colony recoiled from the barriers. It failed to stop their progress, but they moved past Pine Bluff instead of through it.

It also slowed them down. The exercise knocked a full three days off their advance to the Mississippi. Any gain in time was essential, as time is an asset in short supply.

———

The next morning, Corporal Simms ran into the main conference area with a stack of photos and notes. "These just arrived. There's another colony. Mississippi River this time."

"Hell's monkeys," said General Corvus.

"How big are they?" asked Mike Kincaid. He and Evelyn shared a sigh.

Private Dennings took the photos and pinned them up while Simms leaned over the map table with his markers and a set of parallel rules. "Recon says they're twice the size of anything we've seen in Little Rock," he said. "Twenty yards across on average and the colony covers a mile." He double-checked his marks against the notes from the recon team. "Okay, map is up-to-date. This is Bolivar County, Mississippi. West of Deeson. They are along the eastern banks, here."

"Hang on a minute," said Corvus, scanning the map. "Dammit, where does the Arkansas River meet the Mississippi?"

"Yeah, I was getting to that," said Simms. "The rivers come together down here, in Desha County."

"Twenty miles south of the new colony," said Mike. "These flatworms have moved upstream."

"Upstream? Are they salmon?" asked Corvus. "Where's Peterson? We need answers."

"She's still trying frequencies. We haven't found one the effects the larger specimens."

"Then can you explain this, Dr. Kincaid?" asked Madden.

"All I have at the moment is a 'good guess,'" said Mike. "These creatures are ruled by a survival instinct, not intellect. The flatworms in this colony clearly have the mutation, but the growth wasn't triggered until now. They must have floated down the Arkansas River to the Mississippi when they were still small. Some went south, where the current wanted them to go. They died in the saltwater churn down in Louisiana. Others stuck to the banks, hanging in the reeds and shallows. And the more they scratched their way north, the better the water became for them. So, they grew. And the bigger they got, the easier it was to move north, toward the better water."

At the photo board, Evelyn scrutinized the new images with a magnifier. "This area is full of shallows. They found a place suited to them, and the mutant growth kicked in. Hard. The colony became heavy enough to hold their place. When they bud and grow, they push further north." She joined the others at the map table and traced a path with her fingertip. "If this continues, they'll reach the Great Lakes in another few weeks."

"We can't have that," said Mike. "We *must* stop them before they get there…"

"What's so bad about the Great Lakes?" asked Madden.

"We've documented their size increase here in the lab," said Evelyn. "The mass of each worm expands in proportion to the size of their tank. What happens

when their tank is Lake Michigan? A tank with a surface area of 22,000 square miles?"

"I'll tell you what happens," said Mike. "With the unlimited living space and the damn near unlimited proteins the Great Lakes provide, they will experience unlimited growth and unlimited propagation. Picture worms the size of battleships rolling out in all directions. The whole continent - suffocated."

Quiet fell over the room. Some stared at the map, others the photo board.

"You're certain," said Corvus. "There's a hard line at the Great Lakes, right?"

"If they hit the Great Lakes, they become unstoppable," said Mike. "The only thing we can do after that is mark our calendars and start the countdown to the End of Days."

———

One hour later, a hidden radio on a scrambled frequency carried a quiet conversation in a secluded corner of the Science Dome complex.

A conversation in Russian.

"There has to be another way," said Kosta Ilin, his voice soft in a set of headphones. "You must reconsider. The moves you are making are too bold, too dangerous."

"This is the only way," whispered the other. "I'm too close to stop now. I am only a few steps away from completion. This solution will fix everything."

"It's impossible," said Ilin. "It's impossible and you will be killed."

"I'm signing off, Kosta. Please understand - I do this for all."

———

The wingman, Elmer Knowles, spotted the Mississippi flatworm colony. He grabbed his handset. "Colliers... you seeing what I'm seeing?" he asked. "Check your ten o'clock."

Randall Colliers, in the lead plane, glanced to his left. His eyes locked on the grey mass below. "Cripes, will you look at them. I saw the pictures from Arkansas in the paper, but it don't give you the scale."

The last two planes in the finger-four were piloted by Vince Moretti and Ricky Torres. "Geez! They're bigger than our planes," said Moretti, "And are you getting that reek?"

"Yeah," said Torres. "Thought it was your socks."

"Nah," said Moretti. "Your Ma washed out my socks before she left this morning."

"Hey," said Torres, "I told you to stop talking about Ma."

"Then tell her to stop coming around," said Moretti.

"Pipe down, all of you," said Colliers. "We've got a run to make. Keep this channel clear and stay in formation. Follow my lead. In a few more miles, I'll bring us around 180 degrees on a slow left turn. Once we're over the river, we'll make our first run due south."

There was hardly any rain this morning, perfect weather for the Weed Skimmer Flying Brigade. These were veterans who learned to fly during World War Two. They never met during the war, but they found each other ten years ago at the local American Legion Hall. They banded together and created the most successful crop-dusting service in the state.

This week, the flatworms punched a big hole in their scheduled runs. Miles of farmland near the river got smothered or flooded or both. That made for a lot of cancellations, so the Weed Skimmers hatched a plan to strike at the flatworms from the air. They'd

load their bright yellow Stearman biplanes with DDT and bathe the monsters in poison.

Each of the aircraft was decades old, but they ran like tops thanks to Moretti's mechanical skills. Now, they kept a tight formation and flew a course parallel to the river, but a quarter mile to the east. Government helicopters made recon trips to the colony often, and the Skimmers didn't want to encounter them. This was a no-fly zone.

"You'd think with all those choppers they'd be dropping everything they could think of on the damn things," said Knowles. "Try it all and see if anything works."

"The way I heard it is they got the damn things in one of their labs. They keep running tests on those and so far nothing kills them," said Torres.

"Your Ma can kill them," said Moretti. "She'd wear them out and they'd die of exhaustion"

"Shut up," said Torres.

"Enough of this jawing," said Colliers. "We gotta finish this before the weather fouls everything up."

The biplanes made their turn and moved into a staggered, single file pattern with 200 yards between each. Colliers dove first, leveled off at 150 feet, and dropped his payload of DDT over the colony. After a thirty-second shower of poison, he pulled up.

Knowles came next. The heavy weather meant he didn't have to worry about drift carrying the deadly mist into his cockpit. He followed the same pattern, as did Torres and finally Moretti.

The pilots resumed their finger-four formation due south. "Let's be sure," said Colliers. "Same run, to the north this time. We'll make the turn in another mile."

"Hell yes," said Moretti.

"Attention southbound aircraft." The distorted voice came from everywhere. "You are in controlled airspace."

"Ah shit," said Moretti.

A pair of Bell OH-58 Kiowa helicopters dropped from above and flanked the Weed Skimmer Flying Brigade, matching their course and speed. The voice from everywhere actually came from the PA speaker mounted on the chopper to the east. "Listen closely," the voice continued. "We will escort you to Greenwood Leflore Airport where you will receive landing instructions. Flight leader, contact us now on one three four point five. Repeating, flight leader, make radio contact now on one three four point five."

For a moment, Colliers spoke to the rest of the Weed Skimmers. "Looks like one run is all we're gonna get. I'll talk to the nice man." He switched over to the new frequency. "This is Skimmer 210 responding to Bell helicopter on one three four point five. We copy and will comply. By the way, Topper Jessup is in the tower this morning at Greenwood and he's a real piece of work. You might want to consider landing at Ruleville-Drew. It's a lot closer and you'll find Keith Mogens is a lot more reasonable. Over."

In the Kiowa, the recon camera operators looked away from their eyepieces and toward each other. "Who are these guys?" one asked.

———

"Of course we aren't going to prosecute," said Troy Madden. "How would it look if we jailed a bunch of veterans for trying to help? More importantly, did we learn anything?"

New images from the reconnaissance flights interrupted by the Weed Skimmer Flying Brigade were added to the board in the conference area of the main dome. Eddie Beaumont presented the findings to the Kincaids, General Corvus, and Troy Madden.

"Well, they confirmed DDT has no effect on the

flatworms," said Eddie. "Should keep the flies down, though. Our choppers did find some new things this morning. The colony is edging overland into northern Mississippi. These shots were taken over Coahoma County. They're outside the river because they've caused flooding and they're following their own spillover. We've seen that before."

Eddie pinned up an enlargement of one of the recon photos. "But along this section," he said. "where they've moved southeast, we can't find any floodwaters. It's been raining for days though. Humidity is close to one hundred percent. It's enough to sustain them."

"So, they aren't bound by the river anymore?" asked Madden.

"Not as long as the damp holds out," said Eddie. "And the weather reports show it's going to be muggy like this for weeks."

"Hell's monkeys," said Corvus. "We've got no way to predict their path. They can go anywhere."

"Not quite," said Eddie. "Here's a place they won't go. This stretch of land. The flatworms moved around it. The colony splits. See, it forms a gap."

"A hill maybe?" asked Mike Kincaid. "They don't like to climb."

"It's flat," said Eddie. "We asked for closer shots of the landscape. Here's those pictures."

"Farmland," said Madden.

"Yes," said Eddie. "*Satsumas*, specifically."

"Sah-what-muhs?" asked Corvus.

"*Satsumas*," said Eddie. "Mandarin oranges."

"A citrus crop," said Evelyn.

"You're certain? Are they avoiding citrus?" asked Mike.

"The pictures don't lie," said Madden.

"But citric acid was one of the first things we looked at," said Mike. "Doctor Peterson showed us

again and again how that was a dead end with our mutations. No effect."

"How could her findings be so different?" asked Corvus

"Tried to ask," said Eddie. "I haven't been able to reach her."

———

After a page over the Science Dome's PA system failed to get Gertrude Peterson on a phone line, Eddie went to her office and there was no sign of her. Evelyn and Michael Kincaid went from dome to dome and didn't find her either.

They did find an intern who saw her earlier. "She had a hard case on wheels," he said. "I helped her load it into a lift-gate van. She had to keep it level. Said it was the gadget you've all been working on, the transmitter. I helped her get it strapped and off she went."

The gate guard confirmed it. She'd left hours ago.

"Did she say where she was headed?" asked Mike.

"No."

———

The Kincaids found Eddie in Gertrude Peterson's lab. "The transmitter prototype was still in the workshop," said Mike. "That hard case she hauled to the van had something else inside."

"We've got a big problem," said Eddie. He had been pouring through Doctor Peterson's flawless notes. "One of the tanks is missing, along with some specimens. A lot of them."

"Where is she going with a tank of flatworms?" asked Evelyn.

"Everything we need to know is in these pages.

95

She was very thorough," said Eddie, flipping through a binder. "These were inside her desk, and the notes here have no mention of radio waves. It's all about citric acid. I ran a quick test on those big ones in tank six, and citric acid arrests the worms. They seize up, then a few moments of convulsions, then death. No reproduction, either. No emergency budding. They just stiffen up and die."

Indeed, twisted flatworm corpses floated in the tank.

Evelyn was looking through another binder. "My God," she said. "She's known citric acid was the answer since day one. It's all in here."

She held open the binder and shared it with the others. "Look, she's been working in secret. She's been breeding a mutant variant that's immune to citrus. A truly indestructible flatworm. They're in those tanks against the wall."

She read a passage aloud. *Now they can't be stopped. The pestilence of humankind will at last be smothered. The lowliest creatures will grow to save the world.*

The next several pages made her goals clear: Breed a giant flatworms immune to everything and release them into the world, ending all human life. Stopping our planet-killing madness.

"Was she working this plan when she was with the Cousteau crew?" asked Eddie. "Secretly recruiting fin whales to destroy boats in the shipping lanes?"

"Her journals only cover her time here," said Evelyn. "She saw these mutations, a product of warring nations and nuclear meddling, as a hostile reaction on the part of nature. The planet readying a counterattack."

Evelyn Kincaid walked between sets of tabletop aquariums, checking the clipboards hanging off their edges against notes in one of Doctor Peterson's many binders. "But these creatures had a weakness to citrus.

They needed time to evolve, to be strong enough to bring on the apocalypse. Normally, you'd have to wait for eons, but these were mutants. Their structure was already malleable. So why not take the mutation further? Interfere more?"

"It wouldn't take long," said Mike. "She had hundreds to work with and reproduction was rapid. New generations came with every hour."

The Kincaids and Eddie Beaumont carried the news to General Corvus, Troy Madden, and the rest in the main dome conference area.

"Let me make sure I've got this right," said General Corvus. "The whole time she claimed to be searching for an acidic compound that was harmful to the flatworms but safe for their neighbors, she was actually *increasing* their resistance to acidic compounds."

"Exactly right," said Eddie. "And she's had total success."

"Well, she fooled me," said Corvus. "I never doubted her. Thought she wanted to help people, save people."

"She believes we humans are destined to wipe ourselves out. This is her chance to accelerate the process," said Evelyn. "Why wait for the cold war to fail? Or the next war to succeed?"

"Why indeed," said Mike. "With a little selective breeding in a tank full of flatworms, you can skip to the last page and write your own ending. Then watch it all happen before anyone else knows this is the final chapter."

"What about the transmitter?" asked Madden. "Was it a ruse?"

"Yes, because we could have used a mix of citric acid to end the flatworms all along. But it will never harm the ones she's traveling with," said Mike. "Stopping her plan has to be our focus."

"We know the vehicle she's in," said Simms. "Can't we set up road blocks?"

"I'm nervous to pull her over," said Mike. "I'll bet she's made sure there's always water nearby on her route. If she feels threatened, she can run to a stream and dump the flatworms in."

"We know where she's going," said Eddie. "Gotta be the Great Lakes."

"There's too many ways to get there," said Corvus. "We can't cover all the roads."

"Let's work it out," said Simms, gathering his map tools. "The nearest point as the crow flies is here, in Gary, Indiana. But it's all industrial. She'd have to lean off a pier next to a loading dock, if she managed to sneak past the harbormaster's gate."

"Chicago is a better bet," said Evelyn. "Lots of shoreline. Clear access to the lake."

"I agree. But we can't cover thirty of miles of shoreline looking for some lady with a jar," said Madden. "I've got people on the main roads north. They've been instructed to seek and observe, not to intervene."

"I don't know," said Eddie. "Even with a quiet place on the shore, she won't jump out of the car and toss them in the water unless she's provoked. These creatures of hers have been curated in a carefully monitored environment for weeks. But by the time she reaches her destination, they will have been in a sealed system for twelve hours. Likely be weak, depleted."

"You're right," said Evelyn. "She won't dump them and hope for the best. That's an emergency plan. She's got to have a place set up. A little shop where she can introduce them to the lake water. Acclimate them. Then she's guaranteed success."

Eddie dug through a stack of magazines by the coffee cart. "Hang on a minute... there was an article

in *National Geographic*." He found the issue with Cousteau on the cover and paged through it quickly. "Ah! She talks about the work she does for the Shedd Aquarium in Chicago. She's on their board."

He jogged to the main map and circled a spot on the shore of Lake Michigan. "She has a lab right here."

"It has to be where she's going. What are we going to do?" asked Mike. "She's got a four-hour head start on us."

"And we have the Army," said Evelyn.

"Dennings! Get me Anderson at the 33rd Infantry Brigade," said Corvus. "Their base is closest. We need a cautious approach. Containment and control. A commando unit with people who understand stealth."

"Sir, yes Sir," said Dennings.

"Can't she put them down the drain?" asked Madden. "Flush them into the water system?"

"I doubt it," said Mike. "She'll want to carry them to the shoreline and see them swim away. She's a scientist, and she won't take chances on an old pipe, not at this stage."

"She's also crazy as a shithouse rat," said Corvus. "We can't predict her behavior. Madden, get on the blower with whatever department we need up there and cut off her access to the sewer system."

"We'll invent a problem and notify the aquarium about it," said Madden.

"Okay," said Corvus. "I'm going to get a chopper out here to take you and the Kincaids to Chicago. It will take some time to get here, though. Mike, Evelyn, get back to Peterson's lab and see what else you can learn in the meantime. You'll be the ones talking to her at the aquarium. Keep her calm and separate her from her beasties. She's nuts and I know in my gut she's got a plan for when all this goes sideways. We

don't have time to figure out what her bonkers plan is. Our only choice is to keep her calm, so she doesn't implement it."

"We'll do our best," said Mike. He and Evelyn left for Peterson's lab. Corvus spun to Eddie Beaumont.

"Eddie, I need you to figure out what we can use on the other worms," he said. "The best way to kill every one of those slimy bastards from Arkansas to Mississippi. It's in her binders, right?"

"Right," said Eddie. "Give me about an hour."

11

The Kincaids had made their way to the back corners of Gertrude Peterson's lab. They paged through binders and peeked in drawers. "I don't even know what we're looking for," said Mike.

"Anything that might help us know her state of mind," said Evelyn. "We'll need to be sensitive."

"I see. We'll need to be understanding when we talk to her. We need her to trust us."

"Gold star, Dr. Kincaid," said Evelyn.

Static and beeps, muffled, emanated from one of the farthest bookshelves. The Kincaids looked at one another, and Evelyn raised a finger to her lips. They moved to the source of the sound, a row of storage boxes on the middle shelf.

Mike grasped the centermost box, with the intent of lifting it. Instead, the front of all of the boxes rose mechanically in response to his touch, revealing a better radio set than the Army had.

It crackled to life, and the voice on the speaker said, "*Stasya? Stasya?*"

In the main conference area, Eddie Beaumont finished his studies. "General Corvus? Pretty sure I've found our answer."

"Those are the journals of a crazy person," said Corvus. "Whatever you've got, we have to prove it out with a field test right away."

"Agreed," said Eddie, speaking from behind a tower of Peterson's binders. "That said, it looks like there's two things that kill them instantly without causing them to bud or split in their death throes. The first is frozen concentrated orange juice."

"You mean like from the grocery store?" said Corvus. "That's what kills them?"

"Yup," said Eddie. "The sugars accelerate the absorption. And the concentrate needs to be thawed, but not diluted. Pretty sure any light aircraft equipped with an agricultural sprayer can blast it over the colony. You know, like they use for insecticides. The Piggly Wiggly in town has lots of it in their freezer section, but I don't know where we can get it by the ton."

"Dennings!" shouted Corvus. "You hearing this?"

"Sir, yes Sir," said Dennings. "You're not going to believe this, but the United States Army has 500,000 pounds of frozen concentrated orange juice in cold storage less than a hundred miles from here. They got it in a single bulk purchase, then found out the powdered stuff travels better. So, half a million pounds of OJ has been on ice ever since."

"After the month I've had, I'll believe anything," said Corvus. Dennings jogged to the radio and made connections.

"And funny you mention the powdered stuff," said Eddie. "It's the other thing listed here as a catastrophic compound. Powdered orange drink."

"Breakfast again," said Corvus.

"We should try the frozen stuff first, since we've

got access to a lot of it." Eddie pondered for a moment. "I'm guessing you don't have half a million pounds of drink mix lying around."

"I don't, but our friends at NASA do," said Corvus. "There's train cars loaded with it at Cape Canaveral."

"I thought they made that story up for TV," said Eddie.

"Nope, they send it on every mission, and they hand it out to all the VIPs." Corvus spun in his chair. "Dennings!" he yelled. "You getting all of this?"

"Yes, Sir," said Dennings, still tied to the radio. "I know there's a couple of Hueys with sprayer mounts at Ebbing. I'll get them on standby. I've already got jeeps hitting every grocery store between here and Ebbing with orders to buy out all the frozen OJ they can get their hands on. Should be enough to run a test on the colony at Little Rock. Next I'm calling Major Griffis, he's the quartermaster at the cold storage facility."

"Outstanding, Private. I'll get a contact at Canaveral." The general spun in his chair toward Beaumont. "Eddie, grab your go-bag. You and I are headed to Ebbing. We've gotta be on a whirlybird to see first hand if this is a solution." Eddie snuck a look at the map on the table. Corvus tapped a red square. "Right here. Ebbing is an air base in Fort Smith. Let's move. And Dennings?"

"Yes Sir?"

"Get me constant updates on the prep work. I want at least one bird loaded with juice and ready for take off when we arrive at Ebbing. Figure an hour, tops."

"General, I need to speak to you before you go," said Madden.

"This can't be good," said Corvus.

"In private," said Madden.

"Hell's monkeys," said Corvus.

———

The pair found a quiet corner outside. "Something's up," said Madden.

"Something is *always* up," said Corvus. "Be specific."

"My agents have been calling in since we started looking for Doctor Peterson. They've spotted curious people on the roads and in cities all along the river."

"All along the river?" said Corvus. "How many people do you have out there?"

"Enough, but I think we'll need more," said Madden. "These are mostly blue-collar towns. Yet, my agents keep spotting groups in expensive town cars. Black suits and Trilby hats. Out of place for the zip code."

"Sounds like your spooks are spotting each other," said Corvus. "Is there another agency on this, one we don't know about?"

"Probably, but these people are different," said Madden. "We've identified four known KGB operatives in and amongst the black suits. Searching the same places we are. And they aren't being careful, which isn't like the KGB at all."

"My God," said Corvus. "The Russians are trying to find Peterson. too."

———

The Kincaids listened closely as the voice continued, speaking in Russian. Fortunately, both Mike and Evelyn spoke the language fluently.

"Stasya?" said the voice. "Stasya, are you there? You can't do this. They have operatives coming now.

They will find you; most likely kill you. You must not do this. Please respond, Stasya. Are you there?"

After a pause, Evelyn pressed the button on the microphone. "Kosta. Kosta Ilin, I know your voice every bit as well as you know mine," she said in flawless Russian.

"Evelyn? Evelyn Kincaid?" said Ilin.

"Yes. Michael is here as well."

"Hello," said Mike.

Ilin slid into English. "Check the settings on the radio," he said. "The channel should be two, and there is a thirty-centimeter square black box next to the microphone with a light on top. The light should be glowing amber."

"It is," said Mike. "Scrambler?"

"Of course," said Ilin. "That's not important now. Finding your Doctor Peterson, stopping her. That is what is important."

"Where are you?" asked Evelyn.

"Again, not important. Doctor Gertrude Peterson has gone missing, yes?"

"How do you know?" asked Mike.

"Oh, come on Mike, really? She's a spy," said Evelyn. "Why else are we talking with Kosta Ilin on a secret radio in Gertrude Peterson's office?"

"Her name is not Gertrude Peterson," said Ilan. "It is Stasya Petrova. One of my best students at Leningrad State University. It was no wonder the Kremlin scooped her up to work for them. She was meant to be a deep cover agent. To gain access to confidential science from all over the world. But the more she learned, the angrier she became. She thinks every advancement for our species comes at a cost to all the others. She considers mankind to be the destroyer of Earth. So, she has bred these monsters to destroy mankind."

"We're on our way to stop her," said Mike. "We're hoping to stop her peacefully."

"There is a problem," said Ilin. "She has made her position known to her handlers. Now, the KGB is trying to hunt her down. She has made it clear, once she launches the final version of these creatures in your, what do you call them, Great Lakes? Yes, once there, they will not be stopped. They will have no trouble crossing Beringia, finding their way to our lands."

"This isn't about secrets or world powers anymore Ilan," said Evelyn. "Your spy never was *your* spy. She was working her own plan and now she has doomsday in a tank. She'll smother the world."

"We're going to try to get to her, talk to her without causing her to panic," said Mike. "But that will be impossible if your people rush the building."

Silence. Then, the Kincaids heard Ilin light a cigar.

"Yes," he said. "A careful approach has the highest likelihood of success. I will convince my superiors to let you Americans have a chance. However, they will insist our people present, if only in the shadows."

"I'd feel better if we were working together," said Evelyn.

"We are working together," said Ilin. "At this moment, having this talk. However, this is likely as far as our cooperation goes. And of course, I will go to my grave swearing this conversation never took place. Tell the agent in charge - our people will fade away within the next hour, if yours will do the same."

———

Madden held his earpiece tight and spoke softly to General Corvus. "Conversations have happened behind a door that is closed to me."

"That must be some door," said Corvus.

"You have no idea. In any case. I can confirm our overdressed foreign travelers have vanished. The people I had observing them lost track of each and every one."

"What does that mean?"

"It means it's the Kincaids' show now," said Madden. "There's a Bell Longranger arriving any minute. It has an extra fuel tank, and it will get us within one mile of the Shedd Aquarium in less than four hours. Even with Peterson's head start, we should arrive in time to stop her."

"If you can't, we'll have to take a more direct approach," said Corvus

———

Emma Marquand had another sip of her scotch and soda highball then scattered a handful of feed into the goldfish pool. She hollered to the other room. "They didn't say how long we'd have to stay away, did they?"

"Nope," answered Louis Marquand, her husband of fifty years. He turned the fasteners on the last of their ten flood-proof windows. His highball rested in easy reach on the display table next to a stack of "Sure Seal" bait buckets.

Emma Lou's Live Bait Barn had been open six days a week for decades. The signs along the road promised The Friskiest Bait on the River. Minnows. goldfish, penny frogs, crickets, mealworms, and night crawlers. Live by the dozen and guaranteed restless.

The barn was actually a two-story house painted red with vertical siding. The Marquands lived upstairs. The shop lived below. The attached garage held a live bait farm made of large tanks and bins.

The east side of the house faced the road, with places for a dozen cars marked in the gravel. The west

side was on the riverbank, supported by pilings with a small dock for the many customers who came by boat.

A sign on the dock's edge read *Open every day but Monday, unless the river rises past this sign.* The sign got posted the first time they got flooded out, back in 1958.

That time, they heard the evacuation warnings on the radio but decided to stay. The next morning a helpful neighbor in a CudaCraft boat rescued them off the roof. Since then, they closed shop at the first sign of trouble and went to their cabin a few miles from Symonds. Stayed there until they heard the *all clear.*

"Worms. Flat giant worms," said Emma. "Such a fuss."

"Most worms are peculiar," said Lou.

"And determined," said Emma. "Not much of a mind in one of 'em, but if a bunch get set on something, you'll not convince them otherwise."

Lou finished his highball then sealed the dockside door. "I recall when our nightcrawlers all decided they wanted to be on the east side of the box. You remember?"

"I do remember," said Emma as she washed out their glasses and set them in the dish rack. "They kept scooting over, piling up."

"Lifted the lid as I recall," said Lou. "Big piece of screen in a frame made of one-by-eights. But they made it move."

"Turned the box the other way and they scooted east again. Went on for two days. Stubborn old worms."

"As I said, they are peculiar," said Lou. He and Emma surveyed the Bait Barn. The only thing left was to seal up the front door on their way out.

"Hope it's still here when we get back," said Emma.

"We'll have to see," said Lou. "But here's a thing. I tied off a couple of gaff hooks to the dock. Maybe we can snag one of these flatworms rolling past. Cut it up and freeze it."

"Louis Marquand, have you gone soft? What are we going to do with it? It can't be good bait."

"But it'll be a good gimmick. 'Giant Flatworm, Fresh Frozen!' These things are all over the news, and now you can buy a hunk. Bet we can name our price."

"Bet you're crazy. Love you just the same, though." She snuck a kiss on his neck. "Let's get going."

The colony came through in the early evening as the Marquands sipped scotch and watched *Ironside* in their cabin fifteen miles away.

———

The recon helicopters took positions all around a section of the colony in Faulkner County, where this all started. General Corvus and Eddie Beaumont, with their binoculars in hand, had an excellent view out the side door. The film cameras rolled as two Hueys came in low. Their liquid sprayers dropped layers of concentrated orange juice over the flatworms. The moment it touched them, they seized.

"Hell's monkeys!" said Corvus. "It's working. It's killing them!"

"And there's a bonus," said Eddie. "It's killing the smell."

The flatworms flexed, bent, and twisted. This, in turn, spread the sticky liquid to the layer of worms below. By the time the fourth layer was exposed, the next chopper scattered its payload.

There was no budding, no reproduction. The

western edge of the colony was dead. As before, the beasts near the dead ones instinctively moved toward them to feed on their corpses. This resulted in even more kills.

One hour later, a second air mission was mounted with the powdered breakfast drink. The powder proved equally effective, as it dissolved in the water surrounding the worms and made their whole environment deadly.

———

The insulated cabin of the Bell Longranger kept the engine noise to a minimum. Communication happened without headsets and microphones. As they flew to Chicago, a technician fit Michael Kincaid with a listening device. "This is all very impressive, Dr. Kincaid," said Evelyn. "You're like something out of a spy movie."

"Watch what you say, Darling," said Mike. "You'll blow my cover."

"Finished," said the technician. "You can put your shirt and coat back on. Be careful not to foul the wires."

"We'll be able to hear you every step of the way," said Troy Madden. "If things go south, holler and our people will be with you in seconds."

"No code words or secret signals?" asked Evelyn.

"Yell for help. Simple," said Madden.

"Your people can hear me, but I can't hear you, right?" asked Mike.

"Not with this set up," said the technician.

"Too risky," said Madden. "You'd have to wear an earpiece like mine, and if Peterson spots it, she might get squirrelly."

"Hey," said Evelyn. "Who is that in your ear, anyway?"

"My boss," said Madden. "I'm keeping current on our team's work in and around the aquarium. For instance, a few seconds ago I learned Dr. Peterson's lab is in a research building, separate from the tourist areas."

They landed on top of a building in the Motor Row District one mile from the Shedd Aquarium. An express elevator took them straight from the roof to a sedan waiting outside. The sedan sped up Lake Shore Drive and stopped in front of the Shedd's parking structure. Everyone piled out of the sedan and into the cargo area of a large Department of Water Management van.

It wasn't a Water Management van. Inside, it looked like the control room for a television studio. A bank of video monitors showed interior and exterior views of the aquarium's research building. Five men and women sat in a row, staring at the screens and speaking to unseen operatives through their headsets. A sixth person stood untethered to a screen or microphone. She greeted Troy Madden.

"Welcome," she said. "Everyone is in position, wearing plain clothes and stationed all over the building. Audio and video are functioning well. We've blocked every pipe coming out of there. She can't release the flatworms."

"Excellent," said Madden. "Mike and Evelyn Kincaid, this is Charlotte Blaise, my boss."

Her long silver hair (pulled into a French braid) suggested Blaise may have been older than the rest, but the way she carried herself made it clear she could run circles around the youngest member of the team. She wore a black pantsuit. In fact, everyone in the van had close to the same attire. But even with the matching clothing, Evelyn and Mike knew it was Blaise who was in charge.

"Nice to meet you," said Blaise. "I hope our Mr. Madden has been behaving himself."

"Exemplary," said Evelyn.

"Wow. You stink at lying," said Blaise. "But I appreciate your civility. Troy, you should get on your way."

"Yes Ma'am," said Madden. He turned to the Kincaids. "You've got this. Peterson will listen to you, both of you. I know it." Then he left the van.

"He's heading back to the chopper," said Blaise. "Mr. Madden will be coordinating with the teams doing the aerial citrus spraying. I'll be your liaison here."

———

Private Dennings managed to get four more Hueys with sprayers set up at the cold storage facility. The Corps of Engineers pulled together a portable a pumping station that thawed the juice concentrate in minutes to fill the payloads on the Hueys.

"This is remarkable work on such short notice, Dennings," said Corvus. "Madden is on his way in, and he's bringing some aeronautics eggheads to work out how to make our runs efficiently."

"Good to hear, Sir," said Dennings. "Maybe they can scout us some more air support. These seven choppers are the only aerial sprayer craft I've been able to track down. And we still have the other colony on the Mississippi."

General Corvus smiled. "I think I know some people who can help us there. They call themselves the Weed Skimmers."

———

The Kincaids and Charlotte Blaise stepped through the front doors and into the lobby of the research building.

"Peterson arrived about half an hour ago," said Blaise. "Our team already had the pipes shut off. We told them Water Management was doing some work in the area and things will be back up and running in a couple of hours. This is the only structure impacted."

Blaise produced a map of the building and oriented it in the correct direction. "Her lab is on the third floor, here. Her windows face east over the lake, but they don't open. We've also made sure it looks like any other day down below."

Mike eyed both the people behind the front desk. Neither of them looked up from their clipboards. "Funny they haven't noticed us," he said.

"That's because they work for me," said Blaise. "The real reception people were sent home."

"It's a lot of good cover, but she's smart," said Evelyn. "She has to know something's up. This problem with the drains today is a pretty big coincidence."

"All the more reason for the both of you to get up there. This is the key to her lab." She handed it to Mike.

"Where did -"

"You're wasting time," said Blaise. "Elevators are there. You armed?"

"No, but neither is Gertie," said Mike. "No guns, please."

"We don't want her to panic," said Evelyn. "She's got to have backup plans, and if she gets even a few specimens into the lake it's the end of everything."

———

The elevator trip to the third floor didn't take long.

"Do you think they can hear us from inside this steel box?" asked Mike.

"Count on it," said Evelyn. "I think they've been listening since day one. Troy Madden is a walking microphone."

Down in the Water Management van, everyone turned to Charlotte Blaise. "All right, we listen all the time. Get back to work," she said.

The Kincaids reached the door leading to Gertrude Peterson's lab. Mike produced the key. Evelyn shook her head and knocked.

A few seconds passed, then a voice came from inside.

"Come in, please," said Peterson. "It's open."

The lab was spotless. Smaller than her space at the Science Dome. Almost every surface had a stack of color-coded binders. There were several tabletop aquariums, but none of them held flatworms.

"Hello Michael. Hello Evelyn." It was as cheerful a greeting as any she'd given. She looked tired, though. Sleepless. She even wore the same bellbottoms and bright tunic blouse she'd been wearing the day before.

Evelyn spotted a large, galvanized steel tub on the floor near the window. An air pump clamped to its side hummed and bubbled. "You've got the special ones in that tub, don't you?" she said.

"Yes," said Peterson. "I'll stay over here, away from them. Promise me - after you take me away, you won't kill them. Study them. Learn from them. But they can't help what they are. Don't destroy them."

"We'll be studying them for a long time," said Evelyn.

"That tub drains into the lake," said Peterson. "I tried to send them there, but you've shut the system off, haven't you?"

"Yes," said Mike. "They're going to stay here until we figure out where to take them."

"Is that horrible Troy Madden outside?" asked Peterson. "I have to go with him now, don't I?"

"He's not here," said Evelyn. "But there are some people with a car waiting for you."

"Can we leave the back way? The aquarium... none of this is their fault and I don't want there to be a scene."

"Yes," said Mike. He leaned his head toward his chest and spoke clearly. "They will meet us in the lobby, and we'll leave the back way."

———

"Each of them weighs several tons and there's hundreds of them in every mile they cover," said Corvus. "We've got to move them before they rot."

The conference area of the main dome housed operations people from almost every department. Eddie Beaumont did his best to not get noticed.

"We thought about digging a giant hole and burying them," said Dennings. "But introducing so much dead mass anywhere will cause unforeseen circumstances."

"I've had enough unforeseen circumstances to last the rest of my life," said Felicia Ward. "We need a clean way to dispose of them."

"Why can't we burn them?" asked Troy Madden.

"That would be quite a fire," said Albert Sawyer. "I doubt we'll find a county willing to host a giant worm cookout."

Eddie couldn't take the bickering any more. He spoke up. "We can use the river."

"How's that?" said Corvus.

"They're already on the river," said Eddie. "Start your exterminations at their farthest point east and

get them on barges. Work backwards and keep loading them until every one ends up down in the gulf. From there, you can hoist them onto tuna boats and crab trawlers, anything with a refrigerated hold. Keep them stored there until you come up with a definite solution."

"Can we dump them in the open ocean?" asked Sawyer.

"Dumping tons and tons of proteins into the sea is risky," said Eddie. "Imagine if these things rot on the bottom and the kelp beds thrive beyond our ability to control. You might create another Sargasso. Choke out the shipping lanes. Disrupt the fishing trades or the ports."

"These flatworms are a pain in the ass even when they're dead," said Corvus. "But this idea with the barges makes a lot of sense to me."

———

Two plain clothes agents stood outside the lab door. Four more were on standby with Charlotte Blaise down in the lobby.

Mike called to the hallway. "We're coming out. Please let us walk." He opened the door. In their earpieces, Blaise told both of the agents to follow the Kincaids' lead.

The trio of scientists stepped in the hall. "Please follow us," said Evelyn.

The agents did so. "They've moved the car to the back courtyard," said one of them.

"Thank you," said Peterson.

Evelyn leaned close. "We spoke to Kosta Ilin on your radio," she whispered. "He listened to us, and the KGB has backed away."

"Kosta?" said Peterson. "My, you *do* know everything."

All five of them got into the elevator. The trip down seemed to take longer.

Peterson caught the Kincaids' attention. "Which trial do you think will come first?" she asked. "The one for spying or the one for trying to end mankind? My guess is spying will carry a stiffer sentence."

"Don't know what they'll do," said Mike. "But they don't like it when someone working for the United States is really working for the Kremlin."

"I'm not working for the Party or the West," she said. "I'm working for the planet. For those without voices."

By the time they stepped outside into the rear courtyard, the Kincaids and Gertrude Peterson were flanked by Charlotte Blaise and half a dozen agents. The car was only thirty steps away. Every step was silent.

Something had changed in Peterson's gait. And a grimace formed on her face. Evelyn spied a single bead of sweat on her forehead. "Mike, something's wrong," she said.

Peterson broke from the group and made a dead run for the lakeside, fifty yards away. After her first few strides, she cried out in pain and favored her left leg.

Blaise gave a hand signal to her agents. They quickly closed the gap, but before they reached Peterson, a shot rang out. Blood flowed from a hole in her back. Another shot followed, striking less than an inch from the first. She struggled a few yards closer toward the lake then fell backwards.

Fifteen more plain-clothed agents materialized, flashed their ID badges, and pulled out their sidearms. They surrounded Peterson and looked in all directions.

Pushing through the agents, Charlotte Blaise appeared and pulled off her jacket, ready to make an im-

promptu pressure bandage. "Ambulance is en route. Did anyone see where the shots came from? Anyone hear the direction?"

None of her people had answers. She was two paces from Gertrude Peterson when Evelyn stepped in her path.

"Don't get any closer," she said. "There's something wrong here."

"I'll say," said Blaise. "She's been hit, and I'll bet a year's pay the bullets are seven-six-two-Russians. We don't have any snipers here. Had to be those KGB operatives."

With a moan, Peterson rolled onto her side and tried to pull herself toward the lake. Michael Kincaid went to one knee in front of her. "Stop," he said. "There's two bullets in your heart. Stop moving."

Blaise pressed past Evelyn Kincaid. "What's the matter with you? I've got to try and stop the bleeding."

"Look at her right leg," said Mike. Something moved under her bell bottoms. He gently clutched the cuff and pulled the pant leg up. Dozens of flatworms, each the size of a wallet, clung from her calf to her knee.

"Oh God," said Evelyn. "They're feeding. Absorbing moisture and blood."

"Everyone keep your distance." said Blaise. "Maintain a perimeter. We need to contain them."

"My God. You put your leg into that tub, didn't you?" said Mike. "Your last chance to get these things into the lake."

"It would have been lovely," she said between gasps. "To let the water take me. Maybe I'd get to watch a few of these beautiful animals float free and save the world." The next cough brought up blood.

"Keep still," said Mike.

"The world is doomed now," said Peterson.

"Maybe nature will find a different way to eliminate us." She locked eyes with Charlotte Blaise and continued. "We are an evolutionary mistake, you see. We've got too much imagination, and we've imagined ourselves the rulers of nature. Outside and above the plants and animals. Lords over everything... instead of *part* of everything."

Another cough. More blood. The flatworms continued their meal.

"You stopped me. And now we'll end up being lords over nothing. We'll spend our final days walking over the desiccated husk of a planet with all the other species gone. We'll be the last. Alone."

She shifted for one more look at the water. "Some will call that a victory," she said.

Then, she was gone.

———

Two weeks later, the flatworms had been eliminated. Transport to the gulf via hundreds of barges was successful and most of the cities along the river had started rebuilding.

The worms kept to the opposite side of the river, so *Emma Lou's Live Bait Barn* was spared. Though he didn't snag one, Lou sold frozen portions of snapper turtle meat as "Flatworm Fillet" for twenty dollars a pound.

In appreciation for their help dousing the Mississippi colony with frozen concentrated orange juice, the Weed Skimmers Flying Brigade received four brand new Cessna 188s with top-of-the-line hoppers and sprayers. This gesture stopped most of their grousing about the juice clogging the gear on their Stearmans.

After another week passed, Albert Sawyer paid a visit to the Science Dome with news for the Kincaids.

Their project had lost its funding. Crews were coming to dismantle the facility in thirty days.

Evelyn couldn't look at Albert Sawyer. She walked a tight circle by the window. "Thirty days? You can't be serious. The Department of the Interior gave us this site for two years!"

Mike sat across the table and looked right at Sawyer, waiting for him to look back before he spoke. "When you say *shutting down*, do you mean everything goes? The staff? The samples?"

"It's become a powder keg," said Sawyer. He kept eye contact with Kincaid. He owed him that much.

"There's no way we can keep the Science Dome program operating," he continued. "The structures will be dismantled and stored. Maybe repurposed for ranger stations or something. You'll keep all the gear. The aquariums, the lab equipment, everything but the walls. Have your people pack it up and we'll transport it to any facility of yours."

"Are they all stupid? It's like they can't see," said Evelyn. "What about the corals? We can't toss them in a coffee can and carry them away. They'll die."

"You're right. They don't understand," said Sawyer. "Too many of the higher-ups think this all happened because you brought those corals from the Amazon. It's fiction, but it's the story that's winning."

"A stolen cylinder of radioactive material fell into a lake and caused these mutations," said Mike. "That's the reality, no matter what Troy Madden wants the public to believe."

"No one fought harder for you than Madden. I was in a meeting yesterday and Glenn Seaborg, the head of the Atomic Energy Commission, said these weird creatures popped out of your freshwater corals. Troy Madden shouted him down. And I mean yelling. Said everyone there was ignoring the medical benefits of your research. Called them all cowards."

Evelyn finally joined them at the table. "It's because the real story is full of too many blunders, isn't it? They'd have to admit their top atomic scientist ran unauthorized projects right under their noses. And a Russian spy had access to all your secrets at a key nuclear test facility. A major river got irradiated. Then another spy... no, a *terrorist* using flatworms instead of pipe bombs infiltrated a government lab and almost destroyed the world."

"That's pretty sloppy work," said Mike. "No wonder they've made up their own version of the story. But they're leaving out an important part, the ending. You know, *when we stopped all this*. The good guys won. And now we're getting thrown out. And it stinks."

———

On the Science Dome's last day, Eddie Beaumont watched the final moving truck carry their remaining gear out the gate, en route to Kincaid Innovation's DC headquarters.

"So, they've got you sweeping up, too," said a voice from behind.

Eddie turned to find a man with a hand truck stacked with banker boxes. "Corporal Simms! Good to see you,"

"Sergeant Simms, now," he said, turning to reveal his new stripes. "Got a field commission out of all this. Dennings too, he made Specialist."

"Good to hear. You both worked so hard. This truck is my last thing. I'm on my way back to Washington."

Simms rattled his hand truck. "This is my last load. Once this is in the van, I'm gone. Dennings with still coordinating the transport for all those dead flatworms. Have you heard what's happening?"

"No, not sure if I want to," said Eddie.

"They're bringing all those refrigerated ships through New Orleans and carting the flatworms overland to the cold storage facility."

Eddie's face soured. "You mean the one that housed the orange juice?"

"Lotsa space there now," said Simms. "So, it's going to be home to the worm carcasses. And I'll tell you this..." Simms looked left and right. "There's a big plant about twenty miles north where they cook and can meal kits. You know, c-rations. Makes you think..."

Eddie dug in his pockets and produced his car keys. "I don't want to think," he said. "I'm going home."

The End

Trivia

Giganticus Facts and Trivia

- Due to budget constraints, most of the film takes place in a large conference room full of maps and plotting boards where the scientists and military talk about the flatworm menace and possible solutions.
- *Giganticus* was released first in 1971, then again in 1976 under the title *Deadly Worms*. The poster for the latter version featured a giant, fanged worm leaping at a girl in short shorts tending a garden. It was producer Harold J. Kerr's attempt to capitalize on the success of *Jaws* (1975). It worked. The second run made ten times more money than the first one.
- The flatworms grow to the size of beach towels early on, but they are not a threat to anyone until the last 20 minutes of the movie.
- The "Lansen" in Lansen's Pocket is a nod to Doris Lansen, who ran production finance for World Cinema Group. She was known

for accusing people of "digging in her pocket" for money.

- Directorial debut of frequent World Cinema Group screenwriter William Sternbaum, working from his own script. The studio turned down Sternbaum's first draft, saying that no one had made a giant bug movie since the 1950s. Sternbaum added the Russian spy subplot, and the green light came quickly.

- The scenes inside the Bell Longranger were shot with the helicopter on the ground. There are several times during Mike Kincaid's closeups when one of the helicopter's blades is in frame, not moving at all.

- A coral reef stretching 600 miles has recently been discovered at the mouth of the Amazon, where the river meets the ocean. Scientists have yet to discover if the surrounding waters have healing properties.

About the Author

Bret Nelson is an Emmy Award-winning creator. When he's not writing stories, he makes TV shows and games. Over the years, he's worked with Kermit the Frog, Buzz Lightyear, and Conan the Cimmerian.

Right now, he's busy with projects he's not allowed to talk about (that's what the contracts say).

Find out more at his website:
www.bretnelsonwrites.com